An Untold Tale

BOOKS BY
JONATHAN STRONG

Tike and Five Stories
Ourselves
Elsewhere
Secret Words
Companion Pieces

An Untold Tale

JONATHAN STRONG

Z

ZOLAND BOOKS
Cambridge, Massachusetts

FIRST EDITION

Text design by Boskydell Studio
Printed in the United States of America

This book is printed on acid-free paper, and its binding materials have
been chosen for strength and durability.

Library of Congress Cataloging-in-Publication Data

Strong, Jonathan.
an untold tale : a novel / by Jonathan Strong. — 1st ed.
p.   cm.
ISBN 0-944072-32-1
1. City and town life — New Hampshire — Fiction.   I. Title.
PS3569.T698U5 1993
813'.54 — dc20   93-14209
CIP

for SCOTT PAUL ELLEDGE

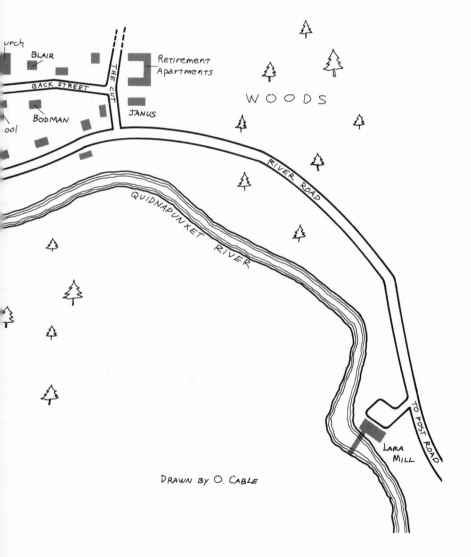

OTIS POND

NEW HAMPSHIRE

AS IT WAS IN 1992

N

unch
BLAIR
Retirement
Apartments
THE CUT
BACK STREET
WOODS
BODMAN
JANUS
ool

RIVER ROAD

QUIDNAPUNXET RIVER

TO POST ROAD

LARA
MILL

DRAWN BY O. CABLE

An Untold Tale

❀   ❀   ❀

Being small had protected the village of Otis Pond from the outside world. In the last decade of the past century, there were a number of such villages — well, still a few, anyway — in New Hampshire's odd corners. Soon the satellite dish would take its perch on the tallest mill tower, soon the information class with its computer modems would seek out even our remote real estate, soon the threatened gap of a two-tiered society would widen to a fearful gape. This was just before all that.

The Otto family had had a lot to do with keeping the village apart for so long. There wasn't much here before 1882, when they built their mill — a few farms, a graveyard, a dirt track along the Quidnapunxet to another smaller mill half a mile down. When William Otto dammed the river's upper meanders, our little settlement came to be known as Otto's Pond, and though it was the less Teutonic Otis Pond that finally made its way onto the county map in 1915, the true etymology lurked in the village's subconscious even to the twilight of the century. The Ottos still owned most of everything, after all, and they had kept us well.

When William Otto had built his great mill, he used the surplus bricks for a little library that sat on a granite slab with the pond on three sides. His descendants always made the purchase of books their special prerogative, so the collection had retained its character over the years: the volumes were handsome and they were old; the words they preserved had stood time's test.

The Otto mill was still functioning in the 1990s, but by then it produced only sailcloth. I'm not speaking of the brilliant nylon (if that's what it was — schooled in Otis Pond myself, I was never sure of synthetics) — no, not the sails of pink and turquoise and chartreuse on a magazine cover in the rack at the village store meant to entice us landlubbers off on a leisure-time approximation of the quest for adventure and romance — but virtually the same old sailcloth that brought the first white settlers to our red land; there was still a small market for it before we struck the second millennium.

The other older mill, the Lara mill, which made use of the Quidnapunxet downstream after its release from Otis Pond, was no longer operating then. Old Mr. Lara had died in the early eighties. His already fatherless grandson Samuel had gone off long before to wander the world, so with no resident heir there were no more irregulars to be had cheap at their shipping door, no more familiar patterns freshly curtaining windows or swaddling babies up in the village. When the last batts were sold off and the antiquated machinery plundered for beautiful cogwheels and armatures, the old granite mill building was given over to the creeping woods to cover in bittersweet vine and wild grape.

As the eighties passed, the people of Otis Pond somehow

sensed change approaching, as yet unnamed, from the outside world. Crotchety old Gerald Lara's small mill had gone under so quickly; did it mean that Fred Otto, Jr., for all his foresight, might eventually be forced to abandon us?

I want to tell what befell us when Sam Lara, the wanderer, finally made his way home. Sitting in the little library on Otis Pond and looking out past the graveyard at what I still can't help but think of as the workers' houses, strung along the curving shore, I will use my pen and these green-lined pages to record what I know about those days. For years amateur tale spinners, more luxuriously equipped than I, have been "publishing" with a few button presses their daydreams and soul searchings, their barely disguised autobiographies on a network (I think it's called) where others of their ilk, who would really rather write than read, may dip in and out. But, resigned happily enough to permanent destitution, I will deposit this sole manuscript here at the Otis Pond Library in what's left of the Otto collection, over there by the south window. I'll slip it between the Byron and the Calderón, alphabetically, because my name (since the spine hasn't informed you) is Otis Cable. In this valley, we Cables go back centuries and some of our blood, as yet undesignated as Cable, back even further. My parents, in their humor, named me Otis, as if to surmount the claim of those late-arrived Ottos who had employed us for a paltry three generations and would for yet one more.

Now that's enough. I shall stop writing in the first person. I want to plunge after the tale that has been held back swimming about in murk for twenty-one years. I aspire to the clairvoyance of my ancestors — some of them, anyway — for whom these hills once managed to hold time stock-still. Let me now conjure up the day of Sam Lara's return to Otis Pond. Let the truth surface, let it spill over, let me mill sentences from it. It happened, as I have noted on the first stiff page of this old ledger, early in the last decade of the past century . . .

I

His restlessness had run its course. It had lasted long enough to leave him half undone.

He must have hitched a ride and been dropped off along the highway that ran on the other side of the low ridge to the south of the village. The bus from Boston to Keene had recently been cut from the schedule. Perhaps a trucker brought him; he was a man of nearly a half century, not the sort picked up on the roadside by software salesmen or admirers of fall foliage. Perhaps in the cab of that truck he told something of his tale, how he had wandered the whole world and was at last coming home. More likely, he kept entirely silent. It was in utter silence that he appeared in Otis Pond.

He must have walked the county road over the ridge; no one in the lamplight of the pondside library looked up from his book because a car had come to a stop on the crunchy gravel, its door slamming after emitting a passenger. Instead, out the north window, where the hillock of the graveyard rose against the pond's far shore, a solitary reader let his glance stray as he contemplated a line of poetry — "The

present dubious, or the past a dream" (a line like that, say —
a line to set the soul wandering) — and saw a sudden lonely
shape, a man, blacker as each moment turned the sky
pinker, redder, finally near purple and the black shape (only
a tree, after all? that column on the Lara plot? no, surely,
a man) became indistinguishable.

In all those shifting hues, unnatural except at dawn and
dusk, the man — Sam Lara, as soon became known — had
stood still and watched the westering sun. To his right,
where the pond's upper arm reached around the graveyard
hill, a light or two came on in kitchen windows promising
supper. To his left, that little library sat like a stubby drawer
from its own card file, the window like a yellowed label
that might have read KH–LA, say, but instead bore only
a crimson squiggle. An Arabic character? No, a red-
sweatered poetry reader stretching his weary arms, gazing
out, puzzling over that human-seeming shape against the
sky. The pond's lower arm embraced the small building
and swung on around under the bridge by the Otto Dam.
Across that bridge, where the county road ascended the
ridge through woods of maple and birch turning to pine
forest higher up, there was already black darkness. Lara
was watching it catch the sun in its feathery fringe.

He stood on the graves of his forebears, Yankees and
Finns and a Spaniard. There lay the father he barely remembered; the lonely mother who had never managed to
control his daring boyhood; Grandfather Gerald Lara who
had always kept to his mill; Grandmother Augusta Thorne
Lara who coddled Sam; the Finnish grandmother he'd never
known; wild Grandfather Oittinen who drank and fought
and kept disappearing and coming back again; great-

grandparents Thorne and Lara, millers and farmers and shepherds when these wooded hills were rock-strewn pastures; the uncles and aunts and cousins at all removes — not one alive now to welcome the self-exile home on that autumn evening.

But he may not have thought about them for long; they were gone. He may have thought longer about the pond itself, there before him again, the captured water. Even in his haughty youth, when he wouldn't consort with certain other boys, sons of millworkers from those cottages glimmering on the periphery of his right eye's gaze, even then he had allowed himself quiet afternoons on this hillock with its worn gravestones, feeling himself held in the pond's embrace and once, to his own surprise, had not dismissed from his presence another boy his age, a village boy named Otis Cable, whose studiousness had won Sam's respect, though Sam himself was no reader, no student. It's a common enough theme, this attraction of opposites. It must be, eventually, what fuels the sexes in their strange unthinking rush at each other. And a prepubescent rehearsal must be intended by the Powers That Be, in that brief love between Quiet and Loud, Tame and Wild, between Bound and Free.

Sam Lara had followed his youth through all its mazes with no one sufficiently attentive or fortified by character to point out the paths that sloped him toward trouble. He was well along them already when he came to the graveyard that particular afternoon to sit, to ponder. Otis sensed this endangerment of Sam's but approached to admire not check him. Sam was wondrous. Sam Lara was the impossible.

And now Sam was remembering that late afternoon nearly four decades past when he had leaned against a stone that read:

AUGUST THORNE
1744–1793

•

I AM SMALL AND DESPISED, YET
DO NOT I FORGET THY PRECEPTS
PSALM 119

And up the hill came Otis Cable, who settled silently with his back against a birch tree. And silence for a while more. Then Otis spoke, loud enough for Sam to hear, as if they were conversing across the empty desks in the schoolroom, which they sometimes found themselves doing, early-arrived and awkward. "When August Thorne died, you know, this pond wasn't here yet. You'd be looking at some cows down there in a meadow by a bend in the river. You think those trees were over there? Nope. That was a bare hill. Sheep grazing on it." Sam absorbed this information and then added to it, but as if to himself: "My great-grandfather kept sheep. Down the valley, though."

Otis knew that, too. Already at ten he had studied the leather volume of village history, compiled and printed by Mrs. Frederick Otto, mother of the current Fred. And Otis had his own lists, stashed in the drawer of his bedside table up in his attic room. He cast a glance along the shore to discern the peak of his roof among the trees, to summon up his treasure trove of facts, of lines of descent, of ownership, acreage, occupation. "The Thornes had all the land then from your grandfather's house past your dam to the post road," Otis said. "It was open land, you know. You try looking in those woods for one really old tree. Even if there were any, they went in 'thirty-eight." "The hurricane," said Sam, to say something. What could he tell this Otis Cable? But Otis had realized he was showing off and had better stop. Silence again, but a fresh mood. Each boy wanted to stay; there would be no "I better be going." They had rooted themselves like the grass, like the gravestones.

It was October, still warm in the sun. Across the pond, the yellow and orange dappling of maples among the blackish pines was still kindled by sunlight, and here the maples were dropping red leaves all around them. Otis wore a green and black plaid jacket and under it a sweater, lozenges of brown and yellow, but Sam had his blue oxford sleeves rolled up, his pink elbows poking the earth. He kicked his loafers off and now from the toe pulled at each white sock, stretched it twice its length then, snap, there was Sam's right foot, snap again, his left.

Otis had watched Sam that summer walk the top of the Otto Dam and leap off into the one sure deep pool, his wiry torso always surfacing unscathed. He had seen Sam swing off rotty tree limbs over the pond and flip and twist himself, landing any which way, unhurt each time. He had seen him bike down the county road, bare feet on handlebars, regardless of the possibility of an ascending automobile around a curve. He had watched Sam do a hundred pushups on the loading dock at the Lara Mill, swing the monkey rings untiring in the schoolyard up and down, swim the pond in moonlight (at least, Otis from his attic bedroom thought it was Sam, hoped it was). But when picking up Mrs. Cable's groceries at the village store, he had also seen Sam Lara, for certain, slip a tin of sardines into his jeans pocket and figured, from Sam's ease in the act, it was but one instance of many. And he had heard how Sam had pounded a bigger kid from the seventh grade — pounded was the grammar school term, legalistic in its way, somewhere between knocked out and wrestled to the ground. He had heard what trouble Sam was in after jimmying a window latch at the Otto Mill, what D's and C's he got from Miss Griffin at the end of fifth grade, how some kids had begun to keep clear of him. As Sam and Otis were the only two ten-year-olds in the village, despite their differences in abilities, inclinations, origins, in the classroom they had always been paired. But now they would have only one more year together in the middle school classroom under Miss Delargy because Sam was definitely going to boarding school at twelve.

Otis had looked over his shoulder up the slope a coffin's length to Sam's naked toes. Nervous. And his fingers picking at grass stems. Couldn't stay still. That was the key, not Sam's daring or skill or disregard for reputation — those things made his quiet classmate shy away, watch from afar — but those fingers tapping and twiddling, those wriggling toes, that ankle shaking, that delicate nervous balance, the awkward silence, the lingering, the unwillingness to say in their privacy what he might well have said — did say — in the schoolhouse: Cable, you spastic, you fairy . . . Cable, you brain, you retarded spaz . . . you fink, Cable.

"Is it true, Cable, you're part Indian?" was what Sam suddenly said that afternoon instead. "Who told you that?" "My grandmother." "Why were you talking about me to your grandmother, Lara?" "No, she was just telling me." "There aren't any Indians left in New Hampshire," Otis told him, sidestepping. "But part Indian," said Sam. "There weren't any real Indian settlements around here, you know," said Otis, drawing on his reading and aware he might be showing off again. "There were Pennacooks on the Connecticut and the Merrimack. This was wilderness between. Fishing and hunting land. They'd set out in hunting parties up the Quidnapunxet. This was all woods and streams." But Sam said, "Wait a minute, you said it was pasture," so Otis had to explain just how far back he was talking about, before trees had been cut and sheep cropped hillsides, before the whites.

Otis rolled over on his stomach, wrapped his right arm around the birch trunk and tugged himself a foot or two up the slope. He was looking at a foreshortened Sam, pale soles and then, so suddenly, brass belt buckle, then raised tensed chin and tight squinty eyes. To him Sam looked big, old, powerful, untouchable, fearsome, but nervous, lonely, puzzled, nearly friendly, too.

Did Sam Lara, half a lifetime later, remember such a conversation? Or, if not the conversation, a vision of Otis Cable looking up toward him? Or, if not Otis's wide black eyes, then simply an old yearning he found inside himself associated somehow with that plot of land? What Sam had said, mostly to himself, but dramatizing it with brow furrowed, as if also performing for this Otis, was something like "I don't like to think about history. What's the point? It's gone." And he had kept gazing out above Otis's head, looking as if no one could reach him at all and he could reach no one else. Stopped tapping, dead-still, a ten-year-old in adolescent despair. He seemed already so beyond the eager hopefulness and watchfulness of an Otis. All the things Otis cared about investigating, organizing, committing to memory, Sam had just dismissed. "It's gone" — a boundary drawn between them. Still, Otis did not feel despised but in the oddest way even more drawn close by beautiful Sam Lara, his opposite. To whom else would Sam have troubled to make such a pronouncement? For whom other than his coeval Otis would Sam have paused in adventuring long enough to declare the philosophical premise of all his carelessness? Were the tears in Sam's eyes — they were tears, not the sunset's dazzle — were they his last childhood tears, and had Otis alone been privileged to see them? And could it be that the dark figure standing in total darkness on the graveyard hill was calling back that very moment from across the years? In his youth, Sam had been all action, all life. He had burned for the next thing as an escape from thought. But now he had stood up there so long, so still. Perhaps, over time, the flailing beating energies in chest and limbs and loins had been harnessed, transformed, circuited up his spine through nerves and blood under burning pressure, and now rushed to the skull, the brow, the temples, pulsing with thought, this dread new resource. It is daunting to imagine, from within, the return of Samuel Lara after thirty years to the graveyard by Otis Pond.

By the time the red-sweatered reader stepped out of the library onto the gravel road and sauntered, as if aimless, up the hill between the gravestones to the column above Gerald Lara's grave, no one else at all was standing there to be discerned, spoken to, recognized, embraced, welcomed home. So the reader of poems, of old novels and older plays, of history and legend, with a few more volumes on loan under his arm, made his quiet way down the pondside path toward a dark house.

II

Whatever Sam was now, it was not what he had been. In the morning he stepped into the village store, a stranger to the girl at the counter. She sold him bread in polyethylene, stews and soups in aluminum envelopes, eggs in Styrofoam, a tub of margarine, a carton of orange "drink" and a six-pack of beer, all packaging unknown in the village store of his youth. An older woman looked at him curiously but dismissed her fleeting suspicion. It was a busy enough workday. The Otto Mill lot was full of cars and pickups, and the whirring of machinery sailed on the air. No one noticed except perhaps Sam, long unaccompanied by such sounds. The occasional clack and slam, the sudden cessation of whir, its resumption, all the daily rhythms of Otis Pond were settling into his brain again.

He was tall, maybe even taller than when he'd last been seen here at eighteen, back from school only to pack up and go for good. His hair was graying now and cropped shorter. The photo his mother had kept on her mantel, the one he'd sent her from Greece after six years without granting her a glimpse, had so faded in its golden frame you could only see the faintest outline of eyelids and nose beneath a blur of hair with sideburns sweeping down then up and across the lip, the faint lower lip and bristled chin nearly white below. The portrait was not to her taste, but she kept it on view till her death and would expressly point it out to visitors, even to the man who came to do her spring cleaning. A few other snapshots had followed, but Samuel as she remembered him was less evident in them, the glaze of his youth worn away to the rougher clay. Though fuzzy and slovenly, this first was her son still. It, and the subsequent photos, had finally been deposited at the village library in a file marked "Lara Family — Documents" kept in the closet assigned the Otis Pond Historical Society. Not many readers delved into that closet, but the key was in the librarian's top drawer, so the occasional researcher could gain access even when she was not in (hers was a part-time volunteer position, and the honor system prevailed).

Leaving the store that morning, which way would Sam Lara's feet now lead him? He might go next door to the mill and reintroduce himself to Fred Otto, ten years his senior and, since Sam's grandfather's death and the sale of the Lara Mill, not so much a belittling competitor as an emblem of survival in hard times. Or he might cross westward to the library, but books that had never touched him in youth were not now likely to entice him in. No, he crossed eastward, hesitated at the post office door on the side of the village hall, then walked on, recrossing the road only when the great mill building with its two square towers was well behind him, and followed the course of the

purling Quidnapunxet. He did not even glance uphill to
the house his mother had lived in, where a former schoolmate had been hired by the latest owner to scrape and paint
the porch railings on that brisk fall day, nor did he seem
to notice that gap in the trees farther up the slope where
his grandfather's house had been razed and, invisible from
the river road, a set of squat "retirement apartments" had
been developed by Fred Otto, who claimed the tumbledown
old Lara house wasn't worth what it would take to restore
it. Sam kept his eyes on the roadside. Red berries shone in
tangles of bare branches, and a scattering of long-stemmed
purple asters, forgotten since Sam's youth, perhaps roused
in his chest a tiny ache. See, Sam, it's not gone, the aster
is not gone, it bobs there, as young and as close to death
as it was in Octobers then, it is still here.

As he watched Sam pass, a sudden calm filled the painter
on the porch, for he was one and the same as the library
denizen of the evening before. And though he hadn't yet
imagined it as he walked home, he had started up in his
bed in the middle of the night, sure that the figure in the
graveyard had thrown himself into the cold silent pond and
never surfaced. He had stumbled to the attic window,
wrenched it open, and peered out at the water. Only then
did he come fully awake, realize there would be nothing
to perceive in a smooth black pond hours after a drowning.
And still later, shivering a bit on the edge of his bed, he
convinced himself that however in despair, however
changed, Sam Lara — if it had been he out there — would
never think of casting himself into Otis Pond. Still, it was
a bad night as the hours drew toward morning. He leafed
through the borrowed books on his bedside table, he
thought of his own years, his own passions, but that didn't

bring sleep. There was nothing to do but get up early, shower, breakfast and get to work, saving exhaustion for the return of night.

It was another half mile to Sam's grandfather's old mill, which was Sam's now; the property taxes had yearly been taken out of the money banked in Keene from the settlement of the Lara estate, money that was his to draw on. Fred Otto had had no thought of snapping up the Lara mill or even its land, which was either too steep and rocky or too boggy for improvement. A drive along the river road only revealed something gray behind a stand of pines, but most people drove out the other direction on the county road, which was paved from the bridge on.

Walkers occasionally came upon the old parking lot, now a sandy little meadow in the woods, admired the granite husk of the old mill with its huge lintels and slate roof, swung back the rusty iron door by the loading dock and explored the gaping hall and the small rooms along one side. The rusted skeletons of looms lay broken apart on the stone floor, and the vines that curled through the smashed panes followed sun streaks around the room. Several leaks had formed puddles here and there; mushrooms found the habitat ideal. The walker, who stayed away during blackfly and mosquito seasons, would venture back by August's close, sit in the warmth of a broad window ledge and watch the light change inside the mill, a pattern of shadows and shapes and gleams. The village's few teenagers sometimes made it their refuge after dark, apparently: some moldy blankets, a candle stub or two, even a stash of certain sorts of magazines on the highest shelf in the old front office.

And now here was Sam, not yet past his manhood's

prime but seared by toil and travel, his brow fixed at last in furrowed lines, that well-remembered look of adolescent despair hardened into a coldness of mien, which still conveyed his pride but no longer his fire. And also something more beneath — an observer couldn't quite say what it was. It seemed as if the ambitions and glories of his wandering years had only recently been stilled and some new deep feeling, vain to try to trace, would lighten his face for the period of a glance and then submerge again.

But the red roughness of the skin that strained against his angular features, the boniness of his powerful frame, these would soon draw the village workers back to him. He was as worn as any of us. From his expensive boarding school, he had hardly launched himself into a world of ease. We remembered his bad behavior: his black Mustang zooming over the bridge, spinning out in the gravel in front of the store and then taking off again with speeding tickets displayed proudly on the dash. We recalled his first wreck out on the post road, then how he totaled the car and two others in a fabulous pileup on his way back to school. We knew which of us he had beaten up, which he had shunned, ridiculed, stolen from, whose bare neck he had held a knife to one dark drunken night. But fear him as we once did, hate him even, he belonged with us. The outside world had not, finally, seduced him, because he was back here, wasn't he, and he looked like us again, his jeans, his work boots, his plaid shirt, his wool jacket, the tough hide, the distant eyes, the closed lips, the strong hands.

The word spread by noon. Peter Doke was bringing his bag lunch from his desk in the front office at Otto's to sit over on the sunny stoop of the village hall when Joanie

Voshell pulled up in the mail Jeep after her morning rounds. A letter had come, she told him, for Sam Lara, General Delivery, Otis Pond, New Hampshire, États-Unis. No zip code, no return address, a Paris postmark. Mrs. Paulson, who had noticed that stranger at the store, had her suspicions confirmed when she passed by, wheeling her grandson in his stroller. Kathee Thompson, the girl in the store, told Joanie, who had come in to buy her snack, that he'd just asked her about the Tri-State Lottery, how it worked, but he hadn't bought a ticket. He had a real scratchy voice, he sounded foreign almost but not really, and he was sort of scarily handsome up close, said Kathee.

When Joanie opened up the post office for noon hours, she showed Peter Doke the envelope and set about savoring her Ninja Turtle cream pie. Otis Cable, who came in for stamps, fresh white paint on his jeans and hands redolent of turpentine, inspected the envelope too and declared it was addressed in Sam's own hand. "It's probably money," said Peter. "Well, I'll confess something," said Joanie. "You probably both think I do this all the time. You and your letters from old flames, Otis. Well, I don't. But Sam Lara's a special case, isn't he? I held that envelope up to the light this morning. It's not English inside. It's not our alphabet even. It looks like scribbles." "Joanie, you old snoop," said Peter. Then Sunny Reichardt came in to catch the news. The two younger millworkers behind her first thought they'd never heard of Sam but then began to recall some vague stories. "Was he the guy who set the diving float on fire?" Shane Troyer, second son of Bill, asked.

During all this talk, Sam, having cooked up a small meal on his camp stove, was sitting in his empty ruin by the river, drinking yet another beer and figuring what it would require to make the place habitable. Some people's memories may have simplified the story since and imagined Sam accompanied by Khaled from the day of his return, but there was, in fact, this first lone day for Sam, which he spent scouting, planning, measuring. And when, midafternoon, he came back up to the post office door and asked Joanie Voshell, who thus became the first to greet him by name, if there was a letter for him and she said, "Why, yes, Sam Lara, there is, and I'm pleased to see you back home," that lightening of his features occurred as she handed him the envelope, a ripple from somewhere deep spilling across his lips, his hazel eyes, his brow, and disappearing under the shock of his gray-streaked hair. "It wasn't the way his face had ever looked before," she told Otis walking the pond road home after work that day. But at the fork, parting, she told him to remember how it had once been for him and not to get thinking Sam Lara was any different now. "Look at me, Otis," she said, and he did. "Believe me. You don't ever want to go through humiliation like that again."

III

If Sam spent another night camped out in his old mill, he was certainly gone the next morning when Ed Forgan drove the village pickup down there and just found five empty beer cans on a window ledge, all Sam had left behind. When Peter Doke came back from Keene later in the day, he reported that his friend at the bank had told him Sam Lara had bought a little black Japanese-made jeep and registered and insured it. But it was several days before Sam was back among us.

After his long hours on a high ladder up at the eaves of what had once been Mrs. Lara's house, Otis Cable would stretch his limbs by taking walks along the river, but he saw no black jeep hidden in the trees. He did find the beer cans still perched where Sam had set them. Ed Forgan, the village refuse hauler, had apparently not dared claim them. It seemed that Sam, unfamiliar with the flip-top gizmo, had resorted to the old-fashioned method; the sight of those two triangular punctures gave Otis a twinge. What a stupid little thing to have the power to transport a soul, he thought.

But one day in that noticeably long stretch of Indian summer, an early instance of what we've since come to expect, when the village was all but certain Sam had only passed through to make arrangements with his bank and perhaps to take an unsentimental glance at his old haunts, Ed Forgan was returning from his dump run and decided to quit the highway for the river road with its ruts and potholes instead of driving a mile farther to the turnoff for the smooth county road over the ridge. He liked to make the empty rubber trash barrels bounce about in back and gave himself points when he managed to spring one out of the truck bed. He'd aim for a puddle, hoping it concealed excitement, and whoop as he plunged and careened his way up to Otis Pond. In town meeting, Ed had been asked to spare the village pickup all he could, but Ed was damned if he wasn't going to enjoy his job; he figured the roller-coaster ride was one of his perks.

That day, after much jouncing, one barrel suddenly took marvelous flight and landed hatlike on a squat fir tree. Ed braked into a mudbank and got out to admire the work of chance, no doubt uttering his characteristic "Well, God damn me!" with emphasis on the pronoun. And then the woods seemed totally still after all that roaring and jostling. Ed happened to turn his head and saw a person, all in white, step from behind a thick birch trunk ten yards farther into the woods. A boy with very dark skin — no, it was a girl, a teenage girl, but not one Ed had ever ogled in Otis Pond, not even among the new folk, that family of psychiatrists or whatever they were out the pond road or those new professor people in Mrs. Lara's house. The figure, in white pants and a sort of muslin tunic, he supposed it was, stepped toward him. No, it wasn't a girl — of course, it was a man, a young man, a very dark one. The large eyes, the smooth brownness of his skin had confused Ed, the thick black hair, the full lips, but was there a faint trace of mustache? Yes, a young man, in his twenties even, serious looking. Maybe one of those Cambodians that lived over in Keene. There were all sorts of people coming to New Hampshire and Ed didn't really know how they looked.

"Good morning," he said, and the brown man in white nodded, then smiled. Then he laughed and pointed, well, not really pointed but turned his hand over in a sort of ladylike wave in the direction of the tree with the trash-barrel crown. "Ten points," said Ed, but the young man scrunched his face to show he didn't understand. Still, he kept up his smiling. "You from Cambodia?" Ed asked. "From Keene?" The brown right hand, now just a few feet from Ed, waved again but now toward the center of the white tunic, and a throaty voice emerged and said: "Khaled." At least, that's what Ed later knew it said; then it sounded less like a word than a breathy cough. Ed cocked his scrawny neck and cupped a big hand to his ear. The man repeated the word. "Ed? I'm Ed. I'm called Ed. Call Ed? Is that what you said? How did you know?" Khaled shook his head and kept smiling.

During this interchange, it slowly rose in Ed's thoughts that this young stranger must be connected to Sam. "Lara!" Ed said. "Lara!" said Khaled, more of a smile appearing, a different quality of smile altogether, one that showed all his previous smiles to have been mere politenesses. "Well, I figured," said Ed. Khaled was gracefully pointing his slender hand up the riverbank toward the abandoned mill.

After retrieving the acrobatic barrel and rousing a few giggles from this Indian fellow or Arab or whatever he was, Ed offered a place beside him in the cab to take the tender foreigner back to Sam, but Khaled, apparently, showed a hint of distress, as if to say how much he loved walking in those woods, or so Ed analyzed it later at the post office. Then Khaled held out his left hand — it had a small gold ring on the smallest finger — and reached for a falling brown leaf. He looked like he thought it was a miracle, those falling leaves. "You don't have fall where you come from?" Ed asked. "Hell, you probably don't have trees. Well, make the most of 'em," he said deciding the man didn't understand what he was talking about and beginning to enjoy his own superior command of English for once in his life. "I got to get up to the village by noon," he said, pointing a thick red finger at the handsome young man — "Well, he *was* handsome as one of those types go, maybe you'd think he was a little flitty," that's what Ed told the post office bunch. What he said to Khaled was "I can't wait to tell 'em what god damn old Sam Lara brought home." "Sam Lara," said Khaled with eager nods, and then he spoke English, as if he'd learned a single phrase only: "I work for Sam Lara." "Good luck to you," said Ed. "Hey, now don't get yourself lost out here. You don't realize you can get lost in the woods. You turn around and don't know where you are." "Thank you," said Khaled, "thank you."

Ed backed up the truck, mud spraying off the tires. With a roar he was off up the road, and Khaled must have watched the rusty pickup with its jiggling barrels and wondered what Sam had brought him to. And then he may have walked on up along the rocky riverbank deep in dead leaves or maybe scaled the higher ridge across the road to stretches of needle-strewn pine forest floor — strange substances to walk on in the strange rubber-coated boots Sam had bought him, his toes warm in the new thick socks but, even at noon with light sparkling all around him, his narrow shoulders shivering from hints of the coming winter Sam had promised would bring magical transformations, frozen weightless sandstorms, if he could imagine such a thing. But perhaps Khaled knew all about snow, knew fall and knew pine needles already. Who knows what Khaled knew before he came here?

The post office confab couldn't precisely interpret Ed's news. "You know, when Sam came in for that letter," Joanie was saying, "well, it felt like he had some mysterious circle around him to put me off. And he didn't ask me anything. Sure, he said I was Joanie Voshell, wasn't I, and I hadn't changed and all that, and I laughed and said no, I hadn't even changed my name. His lip curled up just a little, and he said, 'Then that makes two of us.' But he wasn't being funny, he wasn't even being like an old friend quite. A little sarcastic maybe. Of course, we were never much actual friends since grammar school but I sure as hell knew him. I surprised myself, I was actually glad to see him. Maybe you're always glad to see someone you haven't seen in years, I mean glad just because then you see time hasn't all as much power as you imagined. He wasn't dead, I mean, and he hadn't disappeared in Afghanistan somewhere; Sam Lara was in Otis Pond again and it just didn't seem so strange after all. Then he took the letter and left, just like he was a kid and it was old Pop Nelson behind this counter still."

"Sam kept things to himself always," said Peter Doke, who'd had a brief stint as partner in crime, stealing beer off the delivery van the first summer Sam was back from boarding school. "I never got much out of him even drunk." "As for me I got too much out of him," said Sunny Reichardt, "when he was drunk, when he was sober — all he had to be was awake!" "Okay, Sunny, that's enough," said Joanie. "Of course, he never *said* anything," said Sunny, "but back then what did I care? I wasn't after conversation!" "So what's this Afghan character doing with him?" Peter Doke asked. Ed said he didn't say Afghan. "Well, Afghan, Indian, Arab, you didn't seem to know." "What's the difference," said Ed, "just that he was brown, but somehow he wasn't brown like a black guy, it was a different kind of brown." "What kind of nose?" asked Peter. "It was more of a nosey nose, not so much a stubby black kind of nose," Ed said.

"What you make of it, Otis?" Peter wanted to know. "Don't ask me," said Otis, deciding on the spot to turn toward the door. "I'm going back to work, have to make the most of that sun." But he left behind him a feeling that something uncomfortable had just occurred. When Otis closed up, the others could sense it immediately. His place in the village had its untouchable side. Seldom would any of his pals risk pushing Otis Cable further than he wanted to go.

There existed several such knots of old friends. This one was of an age with Sam Lara, a year ahead or behind. In their earliest days they had toddled about together with pails and shovels on the narrow swimming beach, and later their bicycle wheels, all in a dizzy cluster, were always racing up and down the pond road. But when Sam had disentangled himself, when his impishness was turning dangerous, the knot of friends, season by season, had tightened. In a big town like Keene, each might have found less random companionship, but in Otis Pond there was no selection. And Sam Lara's freedom to move beyond them only made Peter and his future wife Ann, and Joanie, and Sunny Aldridge and Dick Reichardt (whom she would finally come back to and marry), and Rosemarie Troyer (now aunt to young Shane), and Otis and even Ed depend on each other even more. Chance had set off the Ottos by half a generation on either side of them. Fred Otto, Jr., was a big kid when they were small; later, his daughters and son were the little ones Rosemarie and Ann baby-sat. Sam, in his challenges to older boys, for the most part steered clear of Fred, though finally, just before Sam packed up for good, the two of them had been seen walking up the county road in serious conversation, the scions of the mill families, alone together a single time. Fred was in his late twenties and already taking on some of his father's work, but fatherless Sam had a grandfather of nearly seventy-five who expected to run his own mill another twenty years, and it turned out he nearly did. If Fred Otto placed a brotherly arm on Sam's shoulders, if he gave him counsel as they walked, urged him to find his place elsewhere, it wasn't discernible from the hillock of the graveyard. They had stepped out of the mill office together, been obscured by the little brick library and then been starkly revealed again on the span of the bridge, but treading the smooth pavement on the opposite shore, their corporeal selves soon dissolved into intermittent flashes of a yellow sweater or a blue-jean jacket through the budding branches of spring, higher and higher up the ridge, smaller and smaller and farther away, then lost in the pines.

And now it was Fred Otto who proposed to welcome the wanderer home in appropriate style. A dinner invitation was delivered by Shane Troyer to the vine-covered old mill in the woods. Returning to the whirring and clanking Otto Mill, Shane told Peter Doke that he'd had to time his knocks between the blows of Sam's hammer. When the rusty iron door finally swung back, Shane became only the second of us to catch sight of Khaled. "This is from Mr. Otto," he said. Khaled, with his polite smile, held out his palm, and Shane placed the small square envelope there. He didn't want to leave it at that, but what could he say further? So he said what was perfectly evident in the flourishes of Carol Otto's pen: "It's for Mr. Lara." "Lara," confirmed Khaled, holding up a finger to signal Shane to wait.

Restless, he tried chinning himself on the doorframe as the minutes passed, then a sort of growl emerged from one of the small rooms inside the mill. Eventually, it evolved into a language and was answered with softer tones marking the same peculiar rhythms. An argument? No, it seemed more a fevered tirade on the one side, interspersed on the other by gentler incantations meant to restore calm. It sounded like poetry to Shane Troyer, indeed it sounded almost like singing. The gentler voice seemed slowly to hypnotize the growling one, then silence for a while, then footsteps. Shane stood, still breathless from his chin-ups, and watched the white of Khaled's costume emerge from a shadowy corner of the great room. The young man, surely not much older than Shane himself, wordlessly held out the same envelope, its flap now open. Khaled seemed entirely untroubled by the job he'd just done of soothing his ornery master. He nodded, or you might call it a bow, reported Shane, never having been bowed to before, and that was that.

On his walk back up the river road — he'd been given a whole hour off work to accomplish his mission — Shane caught sight of Otis Cable on his high ladder, drippy paint bucket in hand, so he hopped up the porch steps to meet Otis eye to eye as he descended; Shane figured Otis would be just as curious as his own mother and father for the glimpse behind the scenes he could briefly afford him:

Dear Sam,

I hope you remember us fondly enough to come to the house for dinner at seven on Saturday. Fred and I are eager to see you again and to introduce some of your new neighbors, the Doctors Tarnoff-Rice from Boston, who spend most of their weekends up here, and a retired academic couple, Pat and Susan Janus, who just bought your mother's old house. And our own Sue will be on hand. We want to give you a warm welcome.

As ever,
CAROL OTTO

And then, scribbled across the bottom:

No paper here, sorry. Sure, I'll come. Thanks.

SAM

IV

The Otto house sat above the heart of the village on a granite eminence, which had been sensibly shunned by builders until William Otto ceremoniously blasted out a foundation on the Fourth of July, 1892. By the next spring he had moved his family up from the old farmhouse at the foot of his steep new driveway. It was impossible to tell which direction the hilltop house faced; each facade had its door, and the drive circled the entire building, as the only means for carriages to turn on that narrow height. From three pillared portes cocheres, you could enter the cruciform hallway, but on the southwest side the drive dipped below grade, allowing access to the kitchens under shelter of what appeared to be the fourth porte cochere but was in fact a loggia in which at sunset you might sit and look out over the roofs of workers' houses down to the graveyard hillock beside the pond and the little library, seemingly afloat.

If the Ottos' mill had the effect of a Gothic fortress, their residence now brought to the village a gentler aspect, a Victorian fantasy (in granite, brick and slate) of a Greek temple; it was like no other house in the county and, therefore, unlike anything most villagers had ever seen. Even decades later, it was only in library books that those of us who wished to explore the outside world might find engravings or photographs of structures at all resembling it — a belvedere, a pavilion, a folly. From the graveyard's elevation, its stone chimneys looked even loftier than the two square mill towers; from in front of the mill, on the gravel expanse we called the plaza, the southeast portico of the Otto house seemed placed atop the village hall like a crown.

Back in 1892, Gerald Lara, Sam's durable grandfather, was but four years old and his future bride, Augusta Thorne, only two; she was sole heiress to the downstream mill (oddly towerless ever since towers had come to signify "mill" up in the village). And how shabby the rambling Thorne homestead must have seemed and how suddenly plain the Lara house below it, with its broad porch and sunny bays, when once the Ottos had settled their hilltop. Gerald and Augusta, his backyard meeting her front yard in a tangle of forsythia, passed their childhoods secluded from the world of red-faced, mud-stained workers' children, but after the crowning of the hilltop, their houses were no longer intimidating presences amongst our spare narrow domiciles. For where a few goats had cropped the sparse green, where centuries ago Pennacooks had sat encamped about an open fire under the stars, there now dwelt a guardian, in his prized repose, not merely larger beside us who were small but placed on a height and thus able to shine forth, more intimidating than Laras and Thornes, than doctor, minister and schoolteacher, but also protecting, reassuring; we had been granted a kind of feudal safety.

The long windows of the main floor were seldom curtained; the village knew the Ottos were entertaining when the glimmer of candle flame and crystal spread out into the dark night. For three generations, it had been so — William and then Frederick and then the junior Fred — while Thornes had melted into Laras and then Laras had eventually vanished, and when this one last Lara reappeared, Fred Otto must have felt the lost past rushing back at him.

"It's as if we could almost retrieve the old life," he told the man who once a week did the heavy cleaning and, when there were guests, helped serve. "Sam back here, and we're both practically old farts, like our forebears. When I saw him last he was a boy, though I must've already seemed a man to him. You remember him much better than I do probably. I hope he's siphoned off all that wildness by now. One hell of a crazy kid, wasn't he? But, hell, we're all older. Aren't you curious, Otis?"

The man hired to polish the great dining table kept swirling his waxy gray rag, and the man who hired him gave a friendly snort and went to stare across at the proud numerals, MDCCCLXXXII, carved into a granite pediment on the north tower below the empty flagpole. Fred had flown the flag, during the Gulf War and through the rest of that year, but this year it wasn't flying; in a winter storm he had stopped ordering it raised and let that be the end of it. Fred's hearty smile declined the more he watched his view. The hired man went about his business bringing up to the table the eight chairs with their backs of tooled Spanish leather, buffing each with a swipe of his cloth. And Carol Otto came in to decide on the table setting, headed for the elaborately Victorian sideboard, but then she no-

ticed Fred and broke her stride. She stepped around indus-
trious Otis and reached a hand out to her husband's
shoulder. Both were in their blue jeans still, Carol's red
plaid flannel shirt untucked and smocklike, Fred's green
plaid wool one tidily buttoned all the way up to the silk-
lined collar. "Excited?" he asked. "Intrigued" was how
she'd put it. "But Sue's all in a swivet," she added in a
whisper perfectly audible to Otis Cable, who kept his smile
to himself.

"Oh, Fred," Carol sighed, squeezing his shoulder. And
her husband made an admission: "I've been imagining myself like Father," he said. Carol prompted him with a tighter
squeeze. "Well, we've come through a dreary time," said
Fred, "but with these interesting new people settling up
here, and Sam back, and the mill sensibly scaled down,
and only Sue left to worry about and us puttering happily
about — let's not escape to Sanibel in February, Carol, let's
stick this one through." "By February you'll be ready for
it, Fred."

The sunlight from the southwest windows flooded their
plaid backs, the loggia's pillars casting long dark stripes
across the great mahogany table. Otis departed down the
pantry stairs to check on the kitchen, and the Ottos stayed
at their window awhile, perhaps wondering where in the
sun-soaked world Sam Lara had been straying, how far from
the rigors of winter he had flown, surely not just to some
comfortable Florida key. Would he tell them?

And what would he look like up close? Joanie Voshell
hadn't said much to Peter Doke, who hadn't had all that
much to report at the office. And Otis Cable had only seen
Sam passing along the river road and, apparently, was too

busy painting to call out a greeting. Ed Forgan had seen only the Asiatic fellow Sam had in tow. Shane Troyer had heard a gruff voice but not actually seen Sam. Elusive Sam. Still elusive. That walk together up the ridge years ago, Fred and Sam, what had it yielded? Only Sam's farewell to Otis Pond, its failing economics and claustrophobic entanglements, and the aborting of a potential friendship, a relation of mentor and protegé — but not aborting, perhaps merely postponing it some thirty years. Couldn't a partnership be engendered now? Let's think. The Lara mill building just sitting there and Fred's hopes for helping the village prosper without losing its character — condominiums in the old granite mill? Or a restaurant! Fred wondered what Otis Cable would think. If Otis looked favorably . . . And Jim Ezzelino, in Keene, had been talking about opening a second restaurant.

"Mrs. Otto, Judy wants you downstairs."

"Coming, coming, coming." A parting tap on Fred's shoulder, and Fred was left musing unaware. Otis stepped aside, so the lady of the house could take the narrow staircase in the pantry, then removed the tray of silver saltcellars and pepper shakers, candlesticks and trivets from the dumbwaiter and brought them to the table. His employer turned from the window, enlivened by the plan he'd just concocted. "Come into the study, Otis, when you're done. I have to run something past you." The hired man nodded across the gleaming table as Fred Otto strode toward the arched doorway into the hall. The boss hadn't been so on edge before a dinner party in years.

But despite their half-hour conference in Fred's study, Otis managed to have the house in readiness when, at seven, the Tarnoff-Rices' Scirocco pulled up the drive. He took their coats and brought them into the parlor where Carol, in long woven skirt and Mexican peasant blouse embroidered with tiny mirrors reflecting the firelight, jumped up from her deep red armchair to welcome Mel and Patty with hugs. Otis, having taken drink orders, stepped aside for Fred, charging down the hall stairs still tightening his tie. The guests loved the tie, hand-painted with what from a distance seemed nothing but a pattern of gray swirls but up close resolved into the lugubrious faces of sheep. It made for droll conversation until the Januses showed up.

"We parked all the way round by the kitchen door, is that where we should've?" they were asking Otis in the hall. "We decided we'd be less likely to block anyone." Otis, with whom they were comfortable from his job painting their new house, reassured them and pointed them toward the parlor, but not before they told him they'd just like some fizzy water. "With a lime?" Susan Janus had added, as if fearing she'd asked the impossible.

"This may get complicated," said Pat Janus, taking the farther end of the couch. "What with me and Dr. Patty both here, and my Susan and your Sue, we Januses are positively redundant." A good laugh. "Where *is* your Sue?" Pat added. "Probably still plugged in upstairs," said Carol. A not quite so assured laugh from the Januses. "But you mean . . .," began Susan nervously. "Nothing's wrong?" asked Pat, but Carol had just meant if it wasn't the StairMaster it was the Walkman, most likely both. "Jesus, it sounded like she was on life support!" said Patty Tarnoff-Rice. Mel, the quieter of that pair, simply stood smiling.

(Which doctor had begun life as Tarnoff and which as Rice was not clear, even to Carol.)

By the time a single reverberant knock sounded in the hall, the three couples had readied their drinks for refills, Judy had been up to pass a plate of stuffed mushrooms, and Mel Tarnoff-Rice was halfway through a small dish of macadamias by the chair he'd foresightedly claimed. Otis Cable emerged from the pantry, but his ears were misleading him. The knock wasn't from the likeliest door between study and music room, nor the usual second choice between music room and parlor, and it certainly hadn't come from the mill-side door. He had turned himself around completely before he settled on the French doors to the loggia. As he approached them, the remembered face of Sam Lara, slender nose almost touching a pane of glass, presented itself more and more distinctly in its revised form. What Otis had seen while painting the Januses' porch had been only an impression calling back the young Sam in vague outline — broad forehead, tangle of hair, lanky stride, long arms swinging. Now the face beyond the glass, catching light that spread into the dim hallway from dining room and library, now that pale face, surrounded by the blackness of what turned out to be a great cloak — a desert horseman's or a Spaniard's (Otis fancied) — that familiar face, as he drew closer to it, now revealed new furrows and concavities, the small mole on the upper lip grown larger, the eyes set deeper in a hollower-seeming skull, the cheeks rougher and not clean-shaven, the rough chin cut across by a jagged streak of scar tissue; that whole face was entirely Sam's own and yet in each aspect changed. Now the long nose crinkled. Sam had recognized the man inside.

One many-paned door swung open. The sunken eyes wid-
ened, the arms opened the cape out wide where it seemed
to be left spread on air by its own magic and then two steps
into the hallway and before Otis had been able to speak,
or smile, or even realize what he was feeling, the arms were
clasped tight around him, a kiss had landed on each cheek
and Sam had as quickly stepped back and said, "I've never
forgiven myself, Otis." The latter found his own head shaking, but he wasn't sure what he might say: "You didn't
need to" or "I've never forgiven you either" or "Why do I
have to see you again?" or "But welcome home anyway" —
no time to ponder further, for now the suspended cloak
was descending, out in the loggia, and revealing the shining
brown face of Khaled, teeth bared in an eager smile, black
eyes intent on this Otis, this person of obvious import to
his master, even if the English words Sam had uttered were
so much gibberish. Then, in silence, Khaled neatly folded
the cloak and modestly withdrew through a little arch and
went down the stone steps to the driveway below.

"He can join us in the kitchen where it's warmer" were
Otis's first words. "No, he'll come later and get me," said
Sam at the almost instantaneous whirring of the jeep in
reverse. "*Your* Chevy, Otis, by the kitchen door?" "That's
the Januses'," Otis corrected him, "and the psychiatrists
have the clockwise Scirocco." He was closing the French
door, standing to one side, letting Sam lead down the hall,
but Sam hadn't moved and it was conceivable they would
stay and talk away the cocktail hour right there. " 'Clockwise' — same old Otis way of saying things." The arms, in
a black sweater of thick wool, were opening again, but Sam
didn't move toward another embrace; he only narrowed his

eyes, as if to look closer. In crisp oxford shirt and black slacks, which the Ottos supplied whenever he helped serve, Otis realized he stood in the same relation to boss Fred as that fleeting figure from the Arabian Nights did to Sam.

Only after hearing the conversation at dinner, as he passed the silver platter of roast lamb and little red potatoes, was he able to settle on the precise name Ed Forgan must have heard when he came upon the stranger in the woods. "You spell it with a KH," Sam had explained to Mel, "a sound in the back of your throat." "German, Yiddish, Spanish, Hebrew, we're familiar — " "But where you said he came from," interrupted Patty, "it sounded like Gutter!" Awkward pause. Sam said something about the letter Q as Otis returned to the pantry. When he reemerged with the silver bowl of beet and turnip puree, Fred was praising Khaled's homeland as our staunch ally in the Gulf War, but a crackling silence had fallen, so Otis, serving curious Mrs. Tarnoff-Rice, explained what the red concoction was she was ladling onto her plate. "We were far away from that by then," Sam said down the table's length to Fred. Otis presented the bowl first to Pat Janus, then to Carol. "He's been with me a long time," Sam said, "ten years maybe. He was just — a boy. Oh, thank you, Otis."

Sam Lara was aware of the scrutiny of this passer of platters and bowls, this man he hadn't seen in thirty years who, in some matters of life, knew him better than anyone else in the village, better than Fred and Carol certainly, better than Peter or Joanie or Ed, better even than Sunny. Better, closer, more private, more secret.

Pat Janus, retired historian, knowing nothing of local history, on hearing his housepainter's name from Sam's

lips and feeling pleased to find himself at the heart of his
adopted community, said: "So you still recognize your old
compatriots, Mr. Lara, after your many years abroad." "Mr.
Cable and I were our whole damn class graduating grammar
school," Sam said. "He was first in studies, so he gave the
speech." Otis moved on around to serve Sue Otto, who
had been glowing at Sam all evening and now took barely
a spoonful of the puree.

The conversation kept bouncing delicately over incen-
diary topics — war, business, race, sex, politics — but what
might seem common pleasures and general cares elicited
slight response from Sam. "The election doesn't mean a
damn thing to me," he replied when nudged by Sue Otto,
who like her parents was a Democrat in Republican country and fought all the good fights. Sam had never ceased,
as a boy, to batter himself against walls, too, but now he
showed in the curling lip of his late forties only a spirit of
reproof.

When the salad was passed, Sue took none. She had
hardly consumed more than a few finely minced bites of
lamb and now gazed in silence, but when dessert came she
suddenly heaped her plate with *tiramisù* (specialty of the
Casa Ezzelino in Keene) and heaped it yet again with seconds.

The guests were to return to the parlor where Otis had
stoked the smoldering fire into a welcoming roar. For a
moment, from down on the plaza, all four tall windows
hanging in the night above the village hall might have been
seen to emanate the warm yellow of living flame. And then
the human shapes and shadows vanished from the pair of
windows on the left and reappeared shortly in the right-

hand pair, where electricity had suddenly added its colder hue, while the glow of candles in the vacated dining room diminished as, one by one, on table and sideboard, in sconce and chandelier, each was snuffed out.

In the parlor, coffee was served and, later, liqueurs. When Otis was taking the tray of odd fat bottles through the hall back to Fred's study, where they were kept in an old carved oak cabinet, he descried the white form of Khaled through the panes of the loggia doors. The young man must have been quite cold out there, but he held Sam's cloak still folded neatly, making no use of it for himself. How long had he stood there? Perhaps only an instant because Sam was now emerging from the parlor, apologizing to the Ottos for his early departure but his boy (he said) was back with the jeep. "Bring him in by the fire, let's meet him," Carol was saying, but Sam said his boy wouldn't understand — perhaps after he'd been longer in America, perhaps another evening, and again thanks for everything. Otis, in the study's archway, still stood holding the tray of fat bottles; Sam had managed to leave the Ottos in their parlor. He stopped, however, when he got to Otis Cable, who now trembled as he hadn't yet trembled on this difficult evening, glad those were Cointreau and Grand Marnier and crème de menthe bottles on his tray, not empty champagne flutes shivering against each other. "Your boy?" he suddenly said to Sam Lara, whose broad forehead contracted as if in pain, eyes sinking deeper, darker. Sam reached up to his scarred chin, maybe to make some gesture of reassurance, or reparation — but what gesture might that be? What word? Or maybe to stop himself from spitting back his own anger?

Then a deep breath. Then his head turned. There stood

happy Khaled unfolding the cloak out beyond the glass door
on the moonlit loggia in the cold and shadows, an obedient
white-clad form, slim visitor to Otis Pond from those
Thousand and One Nights. And soon, Sam was out there
with him, silently pulling the door closed behind.

The other couples had resumed their places in the parlor,
warm by the fire. Fred presided, standing beside Carol's red
chair, his elbow on the mantelpiece, and then, when Patty
Tarnoff-Rice started leafing through an album of Otto family photos, crossing to stand behind the couch and supply
captions. Mel hadn't reclaimed the chair by the emptied
macadamia dish but, with Sue Otto, shared the love seat
and a plate of mints. The Januses, close beside each other
on the couch with Patty, said how nice it was being surrounded by younger people all evening and how lucky they
didn't find themselves, like so many friends, put out to
pasture with the halt and lame. Pat's quick census now
revealed nativities in consecutive decades: he and Susan
born in the twenties, both Ottos in the thirties, lone Sam
in the forties, the fifties-born Tarnoff-Rices, and "our six-
ties Flower Child" as he dubbed Sue. And if you counted
manservants, each decade was represented twice, that is
unless the Arab was even younger . . . But Otis Cable had
just reentered to stoke up the fire again and Pat, instinctively, cut himself short.

"So what do we think of Sam now?" asked Fred, moving
back to the mantel, half watching Otis at work, half addressing the company. "No, stay here, Otis, you too, I want
to know what we all think." Quiet. "He stings back because he's been stung," said Sue Otto from the other side
of the room, to thin air as much as to her father. Mel turned

to look at her, a veil of concern falling across his psychiatrist's brow. After her shakily delivered utterance, Sue slumped her bony shoulders back against the love seat and would add nothing, despite Mel's head tilted her way, coaxing. "Well, there was a certain sarcastic levity in whatever he said, that's for sure," said Pat Janus. "Hardly the raconteur," Susan, his wife, quipped.

"He certainly had no love for my questions," said Carol Otto. "Did you hear him with me at the other end of the table, Fred? I thought maybe in the general buzz I could get him talking about vast deserts and wondrous wilds . . ." "We could hardly get him beyond transliterating Arabic," declared Patty, still perusing the album. Then Carol went on: "But the more I pried, the tighter his brow got. Whatever he's beheld out in the world, he doesn't think it's worth our care to know." "Usually, you can't shut a world traveler up!" said Patty. "Jesus Christ, you're in for evenings of slides or, worse, videos, and out come the maps, the guidebooks, the kitschy artifacts."

"But it's strange," Fred said slowly. He tugged loose the painted sheep's heads knotted at his throat, as if the evening was over, the sole guest having departed, and now it was just the family. "We knew him before, didn't we, Otis? He'd try anything, drunk or sober. Three girls pregnant those last years, and one was sixteen, Patty. Broke up a marriage or two as well, stole money from his grandfather's till, blasted his damn car down the county road like a juggernaut. His scraps, his pranks, his fits of temper. He'd fight anyone. The peril of the grave couldn't hold Sam back. He was like a storm."

"You're talking about this Sam who was here tonight!"

said Susan Janus, clutching at the necklace of green glass beads she wore. A moment of bemusement.

But Fred kept trying to explain: "He had a secret pride, a perverse sort of pride. We saw it, somehow forgave it, didn't we, Otis? He'd do what no one else would do. And we'd watch. Arrest him? Punish him? But pleasure and strife were his forms of recompense. Young Sam in jail, young Sam out of jail, both still Sam having had his kinds of adventures. He'd have to burn himself out, and he wasn't going to be able to do it here. So off he went to ransack the world. But how did he do it, I mean, wake up from all his wild dreams?" "He's not going to tell," said Carol from her chair, her blouse's tiny mirrors gleaming again in the rekindled firelight.

"But he *has* awakened," said Mel across the room. "Perhaps it's not for me to say, as a man of only thirty-eight" — a good-humored nod toward the Januses — "but he didn't strike me as a former sociopath. A subdued, well-spoken fellow, pleasant enough, a little shy, but seeming to know himself, and — you're right — keeping it to himself. It must be hard for him to return as a tamed adult, but for all we know he burned that wild energy out of his system twenty years back. This is who he is now. I'd let him be and forget the mythology."

"You're speaking as a total outsider, Mel, you realize," said Patty to reduce the risk of offending their host, who stood by the mantel still, shaking his head, looking down at Otis for a word of illumination, but the housepainter-butler-yardman-bricklayer-carpenter was crouching awkwardly watching his fire crackle, avoiding the eyes of all his sometime employers.

"But what I don't know," said Fred carefully, "is if he's actually awake now, as you say, Mel, or if he isn't still cursing that sturdy heart of his. I know what it is to have a *bad* heart, having to watch it, not exceed my limits, but Sam and excess, well, he's made a life of it, and dammit *his* damn heart still won't break. And now he can only curse the dependable old thing when all it can do is gradually wither. And, damn, if it isn't me that's terrified of my own going bust!"

"Fred," said Carol, "we're flying down to Sanibel in February. As always. Don't talk like that."

"But I have a feeling — " Eyes on Otis Cable, who had begun to speak. "Mr. Otto, I have this other feeling. That Sam's heart isn't withering at all, that it's only now steadily aflame, for the first time."

V

The ringing hammer and booming ax echoed in the now naked woods by the old Lara mill; the stand of pines between river road and sandy little meadow (the former parking lot) was like a dark green velvet theater curtain concealing a change of scenery between acts. Sam must have revived or, more likely, replaced the old generator to tap the Quidnapunxet's onrush, for now dim electric light flickered across the granite sills at dusk. He'd also replaced the broken panes and then all but masked them with sailcloth remnants (Peter Doke reported Sam's purchase to the lunchers in the post office), but a faint glow nonetheless made its way into the woods at night; by day the windows looked like great statistical charts, crosshatched, awaiting inflationary curves or electrocardiograms. And behind them the zing of a screw gun sliced the silence of November noons.

Sam was seen in the village often enough. His jeep would pull up to the store, and Kathee would sell mute Khaled a *Keene Sentinel* or a couple of doughnuts. Across the plaza, Sam would check for mail and speak to Joanie Voshell or

Ed Forgan, if he was hanging around. Once he even bumped into Sunny Reichardt coming out of the mill day-care room, where she worked mornings. At first, silence. Khaled, sitting in the jeep, was seen to lower the newspaper with which he was either improving his little English or just amusing himself with photos of football teams and high school wrestlers, of brides and grooms, of the recent dead. His dark eyes now fixed across the plaza. Kathee, in the window of the store, was witness, too. By now, she'd learned something more of Sam's amorous past; Sunny's she knew already as well as everybody else in Otis Pond. Out there, Sunny had started to nod big grinning nods and Sam had stepped back to appraise her, his lips almost achieving a smile, too. "It *is*," she seemed to be saying. "Yes, it is," answered nodding Sam. Then her nods turned to knowing, fond sidewise shakes — "My, my, my!" Sam, too. Then both threw their hands up, oh what the hell, and then came an embrace, not as fierce as the embrace that surprised Otis Cable but lingering, easy, back-patting, untroubled seeming. Khaled had shyly disappeared into the want ads. Kathee, who was finding Sam handsomer and handsomer each day he came by, realized how glad she was to have someone like him new in town. Those psychoanalysts and their three spoiled kids who came up on weekends with their friends and practically bought out the store, and that chatty professor and his twittery wife who found Otis Pond so fascinating they wanted to get to know everyone by name overnight, not to mention that braggy son of theirs who visited with his fat wife and those bitchy teenage granddaughters: these weren't the kinds of new people Kathee — or anyone else in the village — really wanted around. Or those computer folks, the Bodmans by the school, or those creepy Blairs — they were quiet enough, but what were they doing coming to Otis Pond where they didn't know a soul? Why would you want to resettle in a place you had no family in, no friends? Kathee's boss, Mac Rhodes, told her to be real nice and welcoming, which she was, but in a funny way smooth brown Khaled with the long eyelashes seemed like he belonged more than those other people; at least he was connected, and he took things exactly as they were and didn't expect to find some mayonnaise brand he preferred or complain the pastries weren't fresh enough.

Sunny was laughing with Sam out on the plaza. But was Sam laughing? Not really, just stuffing his hands in his jeans pockets, rocking on his heels a bit, nodding — Kathee could only see his broad flat back in his worn-out sheepskin coat. When he returned to the jeep, he gave a jaunty wave to the woman he'd spent half a year of his life making love with whenever they could find a private and sometimes not all so private a spot to do it in. Khaled slipped gracefully beyond the gearshift to let Sam take the wheel. The Japanese jeep backed quietly, turned toward the bridge and, without a single pebble set flying, left the gravel for the pavement of the county road toward Keene, where they would do their more serious shopping.

Fred Otto had proposed that he might wander down and check up on Sam's improvements, fearing they might be so extensive as to preclude any eventual conversion to Italian restaurant or condo complex, but Sam had put him off, vaguely, and from what Ed Forgan reported of the trash set out for hauling, there couldn't be that much Sam was improving: a little insulating, a little Sheetrocking, some wiring, and judging from odd ends of PVC even some plumbing. The mill — or a corner of it — would be habitable through the winter; that was likely all.

When the really cold weather first struck, Khaled was seen rushing into the village store in layers of sweaters, but later that day, after a dash to the new Post Road Mall, he sported an immense puffy down parka, snow white with fur around the hood and fat black fur-lined snow boots. Joanie Voshell began to call him Sam's Eskimo. He didn't come up to the village as often, though. With smoke curling out of two of the three chimneys on the Lara mill, he must have found it a cozy prospect to sit home — home was what it was to him now, perhaps forever — to prepare the food Sam brought them, to keep their little quarters tidy, to speak in that throaty songful language to his solitary master, temper him evenly, to sit across the room and watch with large eyes Samuel Lara's lucubrations in the mid of night.

Sam studying? The same Sam who'd never cracked a book if he could help it, except perhaps over one earnest classmate's head? Sam, whose only volume, heretofore, was lived not studied? Well, somewhere out in the world, the Sam of old had learned to speak a tongue unknown to anyone in Otis Pond — Arabic? Farsi? Urdu? Tamil? Pushtu? Khmer? Arabic seemed right, after hearing where his young servant had come from, yet research in the little library revealed that Qatar was populated by many a foreigner working for the oil industry. How about Inuit? suggested Joanie, who kept abreast of the world's peoples through stamp collecting, her busman's holiday of a hobby.

So Sam knew how to speak and, from that first letter
(which had informed him, no doubt, when Khaled's flight
would arrive), how to read in curlicues and tiny diamonds
that signified to us nothing but grace of line and conceal-
ment of mystery. And now, seeking more to learn, Sam
had turned to the library on Otis Pond and checked out
any number of books, not (as Mrs. Collins, the volunteer,
was surprised to find) the how-to-electrify or plumb-it-
yourself kinds of books Fred Otto had begun to purchase
(back then the literary collection filled nearly the entire
room and not just those few meager shelves over there),
and if he meant to instruct Khaled it wasn't with the old
primers in the children's nook. Stranger still, he did not
turn to Sir Richard Burton or Edward FitzGerald or even
T. E. Lawrence in their fine leather bindings. According to
Mrs. Collins, it was only long poems he kept borrowing:
Pope's Homer, Dryden's *Aeneid*, Longfellow's *Divine
Comedy*, and Spenser, old translations of Ariosto and Tasso,
Goethe and Schiller, Byron's *Harold* and Shelley's *Pro-
metheus*. All those volumes, the most forbidding ones,
which in our childhoods went unsampled when for lack of
other diversions Peter Doke and even Joanie Voshell might
take out novels by Scott or Dickens or Hardy and find they
liked them, those other old volumes, with all those lines
and lines of poetry, now found their way under Sam's black
cloak (or sheepskin coat on colder days) to the refurbished
rooms in the old mill. There he would sit into the night,
at the big table, once the counter at the shipping door where
so many of our mothers had purchased irregular bolts of
material, and there with seven candles dropping wax about
him, he might be glimpsed (on a very dark cold night when

the sailcloth curtain had come unfastened at one corner)
scanning curiously and closely stanzas long unread in Otis
Pond by any but perhaps one other pair of hungry eyes.
And as the candles dripped and guttered, and with the
young Asian curled up sleepily under blankets and quilts
on the bed in the darkling corner behind him, Sam's gaze
would shift to an object by the open book, a white lump
of a thing. A meteorite from the deserts of Oman? Some
sacred stone from the Ganges banks? A piece of the Angkor
Wat? No. Something ghastly, something gathered from the
dead by profane hands, set there beside his book as if to
startle away anyone but Sam himself, an ancient skull, or
perhaps one not so ancient, perhaps the skull of someone
known to him, undone by him . . . The peeper at the window couldn't contemplate further. He had seen more than
he should have.

One crisp afternoon after Halloween in the early dusk,
after carpentering through the daylit hours, Sam Lara
strode up the river road on foot, his cloak behind him filling
sail-like with the breezes, and passing the Otto Mill, now
quiet again till morning, passing Mac Rhodes's store, then
the bridge abutment with its red, white and blue sign —
"YOU'RE LEAVING OTIS POND — WE'RE NOT!" — he
turned to the library on its granite slab, which jutted into
a pond papered now with ice. A family of ducks, soon to
be on their way, paddled to keep a patch of open water.
They quacked at Sam, whose great black wing feathered
down to his back as he hesitated at the library door. Then
he stepped in. Mrs. Collins would return later to close up,
but the place seemed empty now. A sign propped on the
gooseneck of her desk lamp read: PATRONS PLEASE

STAMP OUT BOOKS. The ink pad and rubber date stamp sat ready beside today's list of borrowers:

NAME:	AUTHOR:	TITLE:
P & S Janus	E. A. Robinson	Captain Craig
(River Rd)	Rbt. Frost	North of Boston
Ann Doke	James	The Aspern Papers, &c.
Blair	Robert Louis Stevenson	Wrecker
13 Back Street	Robert Louis Stevenson	Wrong Box/Body Snatcher
Otis Pond NH	Robert Louis Stevenson	Dynamiter
	Hawthorne's Works Vol. XIII	Dr. Grimshawe's Secret
Otto, S.	Wharton, E.	"Summer"

Sam stepped toward the west window, in which a very little light hovered. But under the reading lamp beside a low armchair off to the right he noticed, when he looked across the room, a slumped figure, all absorbed in his book. The man, his old classmate Otis Cable, with his shaggily cut straight black hair lightly dusted white with paint specks, his sparse mustache, his slightly beaked nose and smooth high cheeks, his left knee raised up, his right leg stretching, seemed not to have heard Sam's footsteps, seemed hardly to be taking breaths. His hands, turpentined clean, almost red, clutched the dark green volume up close to his face.

Sam considered what to do. Otis was, perhaps, ignoring him; their last encounter at the dinner party had left a question how they might proceed. So Sam walked farther, past the empty desks in the center of the room, affecting not to notice Otis either, and perused the shelves in the southwest corner. The heating pipes clanked in the silent library. And then, as he removed *The Mill on the Floss* from a tightly packed shelf, *Silas Marner* slipped out and fell on the floor by Sam's feet. Surely Otis had to look up and catch his eye. "I thought that was you," Sam said. "Hello," said Otis. "Damn," said Sam bending down to pick up the book, his cloak falling all about him. "Hey, remember this? You gave a book report on *Silas Marner* in sixth grade." He flipped the pages. "Hey, I remember you talking about this Dunsey character." "How would you remember that?" Otis asked, so Sam, relieved to be talking again, kept on: "I don't know. I was thinking George Eliot sounded familiar somehow. This one about a mill, thought I ought to look at it. Well, now it comes back to me. And I remember you said this George was really a woman. Sort of thing like that sticks when you're eleven, I suppose. *Silas Marner*, hmm, it comes back to me. Locked into my brain three dozen years ago and just pops back like yesterday." Sam was saying more than he'd said uninterrupted all in English to anyone since he'd returned from the outside world. What was it Otis did to him? All those years and the effect was still there.

Sam passed around the readers' desks closer to Otis's chair, his fingernails clicking along the spines of books on the top shelf. At the north window he stopped to look out, but hardly a silhouette of a gravestone or bare tree was perceptible, only the quack of a duck and wind whistling in the eaves.

"Keeping yourselves warm down there?" Otis asked in a voice approaching friendliness but with an edge that challenged Sam to try harder, to answer him tenfold. "In the mill? We've got the small rooms insulated now. Wood stoves. I've seen a lot worse than a New Hampshire winter

over the years. Still, I don't welcome it." "Your boy, too?"
Otis had used that dangerous-seeming word. But then, perhaps it wasn't the "boy" that had set Sam off as much as
the "your" — "More of a young man, I put it wrong before,
I'm sorry, Otis," Sam said. Had that cleared it up? Otis
only shrugged. But, of course, it wasn't the "your" or the
"boy" that had unsettled his childhood friend, it was both
words together. In all his life only one other person had
ever been Sam's boy, as village whisperings once phrased
it, and how brief and how sad and how cruel that time of
possession had been. Sam studied the man, with left knee
now hooked over the chair arm as a sixth grader might
have sat, book open in his lap, a scowl underlining what
resembled the very first mustache Sam himself ever at-
tempted, at eighteen, just before he left Otis Pond. His
Indian blood, Sam thought. Well, maybe if we keep talking . . . "Surprised to see me in this old library?" "I expected you'd come in, one of these afternoons. Your name's
been on the list before." "Surprised?" "A lot's different
about you now, Lara," Otis said, but not as a question, and
then went on: "Funny how you aren't exactly sure who
George Eliot was but you're signing out all that epic poetry." A hint of the old show-off Otis Cable from sixth
grade? Or genuine curiosity? "I like it being in lines," Sam
said, a simple truth he supposed made him sound stupid.
"Those fat paragraphs in novels, I can't face them." Otis
almost smiled. "But what's that there? It's in lines," Sam
said. He turned from the window and bent over Otis's
shoulder to read the title at the top of a page, *Secret Vengeance for Secret Insult*, but didn't say it aloud. Otis
snapped the book shut, explained it was an old Spanish

tragedy by Calderón, but instead of discoursing further, he returned to his former theme: "I never heard of anyone finding epic poetry easier to read than novels." Otis wasn't really being snooty; he was just Otis as Sam had always remembered him. Sam imagined his old classmate managing over the years to read every damn book in that library. And now Otis was asking, whether or not with an edge of condescension: "But what makes you want to read at all, Lara?"

How to answer him? "I have trouble sleeping" was what Sam came back with; then he added, "I can have a hell of a night sometimes," but he'd better leave it at that, he thought. So he stepped over to the front desk and signed "Lara, S." to conform with the previous borrower's style. "You giving George Eliot a try?" Otis called across to him. "Will it put me right to sleep?" Sam joked back. A shrug from the armchair. "Oh well, it's about a mill," Sam said. "Mary Ann Evans — that was her name — she wasn't the only one," said Otis, "the Brontë sisters over there were the Bell brothers for a while." Now what could Sam tell Otis Cable in return? How Tancred was spurned by Clorinda, who dressed in the armor of a man? It was a good story — but Cable probably knew it by heart. Sam was pulling his cloak around him when it occurred to him he might instead say something concerning what his hostess of a few weeks back had told him, quietly, at their corner of the dinner table. Would mentioning it show Otis a measure of respect, or would it hurt? No, Sam shouldn't be so careful. With Otis he should always just speak.

"Carol told me that you had been living with a friend, Otis. I wish somehow I'd made it back sooner — I mean, to have known him. I'm sorry if it ended."

Otis raised his head into the lamplight looking at Sam with a dark clairvoyant stare. "There have been several that ended," he said.

The sentence went through Sam and bounced back at him from the southeast corner, the children's nook, and Sam could only shake his head sadly, then nod, the way he'd been seen nodding to Sunny Reichardt out on the plaza. We all know each other, have known all of each other, and it has been such a long sad time, and what can be said now? — These unspoken words hovered in the stuffy moldy breathing space between the two men. Did they both understand them the same way?

VI

It was night. Stars studded the glassy stream above the crumbling old Lara dam, each beam from far in the universe finding its path to a twinkling image on our autumn-stilled Quidnapunxet. The water scarcely seemed to move, so calm and dry the weather had been, and yet under there, pressing against the concrete, pouring through sluiceways, it did move — enough to supply a thread of electricity — and it kept moving, like happiness, away.

The bare trees, which provided goodly shade in summer, now netted stars, those lights along the sky that lived forever. Hunters and fishers a millennium ago had watched them, too, but gave them other names than ours. Underfoot, now only low moss and shriveling ferns kept green, but at night within the blackness green persisted, incipient, immanent, even in the waning year. The mazy winding channel, like a snake, threaded its way between the banks, ignoring backwaters, shunning the calmer surface, pulsing always downward. On such a still night, with winter coming but not yet there, it would not startle you to meet a spirit in those woods, an old Indian woman wise as the stars who has inhabited this land over centuries and now appears, there by a birch trunk in moonlight, to comfort a remnant of her tribe, night-walking to calm his soul but finding himself only deeper in darkness. Others — two teenagers, all bundled up — had snuck out earlier into the night with illicit purposes, but the wise spirit had greeted them, too, and stretched out her arms like sheltering hemlock boughs over them both. Just in time — for yet another noctambulist was passing.

If Sam should have chanced upon them, their tryst would have reminded him of a time when nights like this one seemed to come more frequently, under more blazing moons in more cloudless skies. Now, if it were storming, Sam would be out in it, wind and rain beating his brow, unfelt, unsparing, but this soft lingering remnant of autumn could only mock a memory in his breast. And so, descending the river road on foot, after a somewhat awkward evening in the house of his childhood listening to the pair of Januses rattle on about themselves in hopes of drawing forth reciprocal revelations, Sam headed quickly for the winking light behind the pines and gratefully lifted the iron door latch to step into his silent hall, that boneyard of disassembled looms.

When he opened the door to his small study, a kerosene lamp within shot his high shadow back along the far wall of the great room. Khaled sat at Sam's desk, before him the file marked "Lara Family — Documents" which Sam had repossessed from the library that very afternoon when he'd gone to return, half unread, *The Mill on the Floss* and borrowed instead another of his preferred epics, Fanshawe's translation of *The Lusiads*.

Khaled's dark eyes had filled with delight at each old photo that fell out from among indecipherable pages of Roman alphabet in pen and type and penciled scrawl. At last, he could see the faces that once encased the souls of Sam's ancestors: the second August Thorne and Achsah his wife; Erastus Thorne; James and Sarah; Elias who built the mill; Augusta's parents Samuel and Grace (who died in childbirth at twenty); Augusta and Gerald Lara themselves, in all seasons of their lives, from long-skirted babies to shabby oldsters: Augusta tottering across the lawn to an eightieth birthday picnic, Gerald gaping in anguish beside her deathbed a year later; on the Lara side, only one peek at the Spanish forebear but many a Lara since — Gerald's parents, his sisters, their offspring scattered about the country; and of the Finns a quantity of Oittinens and even Sam's mother's mother, suffering wife of a wild old man, her cow eyes staring out at Khaled as if to say, "There was nothing in life for me, nothing at all, I didn't even outlast him." These pictures were the evidence, for Khaled to assess, of the virtues and crimes of his master's folk. Each face, surely, would reveal an element of Sam's destiny if it could be conned aright. In the senior Mrs. Frederick Otto's history of the village, the Laras took up a good half chapter, but the specious tale she told of them, even if Khaled could have read it, would have disclosed fewer truths than now glinted in those old photographs.

And the photos of Sam himself — well, it made Khaled's hands fairly tremble to hold them. The one Sam's mother used to display on her mantelpiece, that photo so bleached by time showing vagabond Sam on a Greek island, seemed not a glimpse into history so much as Sam's very presence nearing Khaled for the first time, nearing the sands of his homeland when he was just born, a spirit of Sam Lara, angel guardian, hovering to the west across white deserts and winy seas, already coexisting under the same sweltering sun with the small brown baby in Qatar; Khaled now held the proof of this in his hands. And there in the doorframe was the same Sam come home to him. Did he go hold him in welcoming arms, lead him to that bed piled high with quilts and blankets?

But how could it be that a teenage Sam, who once coaxed girls to lie with him along the flower-fringed stream, who had once met in the light of the moon with a boy his own age and held a silver blade to his throat, how could that young Sam have become this Sam of poetry, this Sam with this Khaled, back here, accompanied like this, compounding the insult of the past?

It was midnight. The moon had soared high enough now to cast its beam across the blind windows of the mill. The sailcloth inside must have spread a dim glow over the stone floor and high-fretted roof of the great room. And Sam, his bristling gray locks, his gloomy brow, his cloak now falling from his shoulders, must have seemed a specter as he shut again the door of the warm little inner room and turned down the lamp. Soon all was slumber.

The Indian spirit woman was moving about the woods. Her feet did not touch earth. The branches of hemlocks and pines rustled when she passed, the barren maples whistled in the wake of her passing. The teenage lovemakers murmured to each other, suspecting her presence. But the lone tribesman knew her, spoke with her, because she had always known him and counseled him. Watchfulness was her counsel and patience with the unfolding of time. The eventual lies already within the husk, she said. The husk will split, will splinter, new green will root and grow. He knew that, could wait, could watch, and in the meantime ponder. Still, he needed to sense her there, assuring him, because despite what he knew he was also alone — and never so alone as when he perceived the spot of lamplight on the shade go dim, as if now loath to break the night.

Something whirring, then a motor's chug and thunk — that was behind him, out on the road. And then a minute more and from inside the dark mill rose a shriek, trapped in granite, then a fearful call, and again one long loud shriek and its frantic echo. Someone's footsteps now pounded the sand across the little meadow running toward the mill's loading dock. A leap, a god damn, and thuds on the iron door, a light on inside suddenly, electric brightness as the door swung open. "What was that god damn screaming? Heard it way out on the road. Oh, forget it, you can't understand what I'm saying. Let me in."

The door stood open after the two shapes rushed inside. Then, two others emerged from around behind by the mill pond, hesitant to approach, quickly zipping coats up over their bared chests. The moon shone on the faces, Shane Troyer's and Emmy Grandy's. They took each other's hands and whispered close. They stepped forward, listened, retreated to shadow, then whispered more, and decided, moved, were up on the dock, at the door, calling, stepping inside where Sam Lara was stretched out on the cold stone clenching the hilt of a knife in his right hand.

So in the morning Ed Forgan had plenty to report; it couldn't wait till noon. He caught Joanie as she was hopping into her Jeep to get the mail in Keene; he snagged Otis walking toward the Januses' for his last day of the final coat of paint; he dragged them both to the mill office where Peter was sure to be, already at this early hour, and where Sunny would pop in before opening up the day-care room.

"His face looked like he wanted to kill," Ed told them. "Then he sees me, so he drops the knife. I guess it wasn't me he was after. His eyebrows were way up like he's warning me stay back. And he's trying to say something that's not coming out his mouth. That Khaled's probably thinking he's took a fit and bit the big cookie. But Sam's taking a breath, you could see, a breath and a breath, just barely."

Peter Doke had the notion Ed's truck making a racket up the road woke Sam from a nightmare and it took him a while to realize he was back in his mill, not in some Kurdish village getting strafed by Saddam Hussein. "So now I'm god damn Saddam Hussein," Ed sniffed. "But what were you saying about Shane and the Grandy girl?" Joanie wanted to know. "I told you they showed up, too." "Busy night in those woods," said Joanie. "Well, I'm in there with that Khaled and he can't understand what I'm saying and, big surprise, in come those two horndogging kids. See, I seen them earlier heading off down the road." "So you were out horndogging yourself," said Joanie. They all knew Ed's penchant for monitoring the love life of the young but had given up expecting him to cut it out. "Aw, Joanie," Ed said, "why don't you go to Keene and pick up the U.S. Female?" "Hey," snapped Peter, "come on, back to the story, Ed." But Ed had decided to scratch the loose skin on his neck and let them wait.

Then Sunny came in and had to be caught up. "You tell

her, bigmouth Joanie," Ed said. But when it was his turn to carry the story further, he put the portrait he'd been studying of Ann Doke and the kids back on Peter's desk and strolled to the sliding window over the mill's first floor. "Shop's open," he said. "There's Emmy Grandy at her stitcher yawning like a son of a bitch. So anyways, they were there, those two kids, and the three of us get under him and raise him up. That wacky Iraqi just stood around looking dumb. And we sling Sam onto his bed. I can tell you, pals, there's only one bed in that mill, and it's just about wide enough for two if you're real cozy. So the Arab either sleeps on the floor like a slave boy or — " "Come on, Ed," said Peter, leaning back in his desk chair, feet up, head shaking, and Joanie came out with "Ed, you probably have your eye at their keyhole every night, so don't get Christian on us now." Ed pulled on his earlobes as if to wag them at Peter when he caught him exchanging a glance with Joanie. "So don't you want to hear some more?" Ed said. "Otis, you ain't sassing me. What's wrong with you? You want to hear more about your old Sam?"

"Sam's all right now," Otis said. The sequence felt entirely familiar to Otis, who had suffered more than Sam through the brawls, accidents, romances, arrests, flights that constituted the adventure novel of Sam's adolescence.

"Yeah, he's all right, but first I wasn't sure. His face gets back a little color, but then his eyes start rolling around in his head, then his legs start shaking, and Shane and me are holding him down and Emmy's backing up against the wall 'cause it's getting creepy. Then Sam starts talking gobbledygook. He's looking at us thinking we know what he's going on about, but it just sounds like he's trying to quid something up." Here Ed made some peculiar sounds for his friends' amusement. "Well, I should've known it was just Arabian. That kid Khaled comes back over from wherever he was hiding and bends down to Sam's ear and starts blabbing Arabian back to him. Peter, you're full of bullshit. The only thing my truck scared was Shane Troyer's tool. You think old Sam's scared like that from just a dream?"

"Listen to us going on about Sam," said Peter, organizing the billing slips on his desk like he was getting ready for work. "Tell you what," he said, "let's get that Dr. Turn-Off-the-Rice to do his number on him and spare us the effort." "Sam wouldn't go to any shrink," Sunny said. "It's years too late anyway for shrinking Sam," said Joanie.

But Sunny had to dash out when she heard some little kids squealing on the plaza, Otis had to finish up the Janus job and Joanie was running late — "Don't forget to get yourself a nice jelly doughnut over in Keene," said Ed, who didn't have to be anywhere, but Peter kicked him out anyway. "I tell you," said Ed, "with friends like you guys, who needs Jesus?"

VII

The village was amazed in the weeks toward Thanksgiving, when Sam would cross the plaza to library or store or post office or take an amble through the graveyard, how no word or look or gesture betrayed his recollection of that night. With Sam's senses restored, the memory had apparently vanished, and only the gloom lingered, not to be unraveled. Even Ed Forgan didn't want to try mentioning anything to Sam now, and the villagers were left wondering if anything at all had happened, if it wasn't *our* dream that Sam's cry had broken the slumbering night, that his oppressed and overlabored brain had gone whirling for a fevered moment, that his voice had wildly poured forth Arabic in an unintelligible drama behind a closed curtain.

But Shane Troyer had heard and seen; if for Shane's elders an aura protected Sam from inquisition, Shane judged him no such kind of mythic character. The following afternoon he went to find Otis, who was cleaning up after the job at the Janus house; Shane had to talk to him. "It was weird, Otis. I could see Khaled wanted us out of there once Sam started talking. But Ed couldn't pass up a chance for some good snooping. There wasn't much — a pile of library books and, get this, a human skull right on Sam's desk. Emmy's freaking at that because she reads too much Stephen King." "Reads who?" Otis asked. Shane rolled his eyes. "Don't you ever get over to Keene, Otis? You never leave town, do you!" "Occasionally," Otis claimed, but Shane didn't believe him. "So anyway, I made Ed hurry and drive us back up home." Otis was recapping two paint buckets, tamping the rims of their lids firmly into the grooves and wiping the lips with his rag, not all that interested in Shane's recital. "Listen, Otis, I'm an okay guy, aren't I? Can I ask you something?" A nod. "You know I realized about you and Mr. Landes. I mean, the kids all knew, it was no big deal, right?" "No big deal," said Otis with a crinkle of a smile. "I liked Mr. Landes, too," Shane continued, anxious not to offend, but he had to ask his question: "So this thing with Sam Lara and Khaled, I mean, it's definitely gay, isn't it?" Otis made a gesture with eyebrows and fingertips that seemed to mean, "How dense can this boy get!" "But wasn't Sam supposed to be the village stud back when?" "Don't worry, Shane," Otis said, giving him a long mock-serious stare, "no one doubts your own immutable heterosexuality." "Otis, you crack me up," said Shane, not entirely sure what the housepainter meant, but he didn't want to seem any more out of it than he already feared he was, so he kept on: "But with Sam, I mean, it isn't like with you and Mr. Landes. You were just two guys that everyone got along with. But Sam and this Khaled, I don't know . . ."

Otis took a seat on the broad glistening maroon porch

steps, unscuffed, unchipped — nothing like the first few weeks of a fresh paint job. He tapped the stair beside him, so Shane sat down, too. The boy was the age of Otis and Sam when Sam left town, but Shane wasn't one ever to make Sam's kind of trouble: he'd do well at the mill, and so would Emmy — they'd marry and have two children, and things would only start going rotten for them later, when Emmy was tubby and Shane nearly bald. In his eager youth, he kept his slightly red hair brushed up from his forehead; it was short enough to stand on its own, or maybe there was something gooey in there, like Wildroot Creme Oil in refined form. Shane's face, Otis realized, was entirely smooth, the way he had still envisioned the faces of his contemporaries before Sam's return caused him at last to admit their emerging irregularities.

Now Otis watched the blood surface in his rough hands as he rubbed the turp rag over them and then picked at the white residue under his fingernails. "Well, here's a handyman's psychology for you, Shane," he said. "My father taught me to fix things. I had to take a thing slowly apart, watching carefully, and think, and then decide what was wrong. He started me on simple things — clogged gutters, leaky faucets, shorts in the wiring. I got good at things, bit by bit. That's the way I read, too. I don't know this King that Emmy reads, but she reads — that's good. You're not a reader, I can tell, so how are you going to know people? There's not enough of them to watch in Otis Pond." "I go over to Keene," said Shane, punching at Otis's elbow with a karate grunt. "So what's this handyman's psychology again?" "Well, apply it to me," said Otis. "No, I won't embarrass you, Shane, you don't have to hear any unsettling secrets. But you thought Landes and I were just fine. Must've been something wrong, though, or why did Landes move on? And Sam and Khaled look — weird? It's not because of the seizure, whatever it was, though; it's how this Khaled acts somehow more like a girl, isn't it?" Otis watched the redness flushing up Shane's neck to his cheeks and temples. "I didn't figure on saying so, but I guess," he told Otis. "Don't worry it so damn much," Otis said. "If you'd read a book once in a while, you'd see there's all kinds in the world out there. That's why the Ottos gave us that library, you know, since we're all likely to stay stuck here. If you read, who needs to travel? And you might just understand a few things if they come your way."

Shane's blush was sinking into his collar; it wasn't so tricky, after all, talking about all this with Otis, but just in case, he added: "Hey, I didn't mean there's anything *wrong* with Khaled acting more like a girl." "No, we'll leave that thought to the Christians," said Otis. Shane nodded, unused to swipes against his religion and surprised at the sense of solidarity he suddenly felt with Otis Cable. It might be more fun being a grown-up among grown-ups than he'd realized. You could talk to older people, even the ones you wouldn't hang out with if they were your age, and you could say things and know things and not wonder what other kids thought of you. His older brother Barrett always said, "Shane, you'll see for yourself someday." Barrett applied it to everything they disagreed about, getting the future Shane to ally with him against Shane himself, two to one. But now Shane *was* seeing.

Which led him to want to ask another question, too personal or not. He had to work up to it, because he liked

Otis and didn't want to make him sore, but it was also because he liked him that he finally found himself saying, "But isn't it weird for you, somehow, I mean, to have Sam Lara coming back here and turning out to be gay? Hey, Otis?"

Otis had put his head down and was staring at the step below. "I mean, *you* had to be all alone then. Aunt Rosemarie was telling us when she was up last weekend how you really used to be in love with Sam, everybody figured as much. You took a lot of crap, right?" Otis's lips puckered under his thin mustache as he considered the past. "Kids don't know what's happening to them most of the time," he said. "Be glad you're over your kid stage, Shane. Now you can spend your life making up for it." Shane laughed and gave Otis's shoulder a brisk tug. Then Susan Janus peeked out the door to see if her housepainter wanted any tea, and your young friend there, she added. "No thanks, we're just sitting after work, Mrs. Janus." "A beer instead?" "Well, now you mention it . . ." Soon they had their beers in tall glasses with a quarter of a lime floating in each, which put them off a bit but neither said anything but thanks. Susan would have liked to sit and chat with them, but she didn't feel easy enough yet with that sort of village colloquy, so she said it was a little chilly out for her and withdrew from her own front porch.

"I like your handyman's philosophy," Shane said. "Psychology," Otis corrected him. "Oh yeah, psychology." Shane had squeezed the lime and decided he liked it with the beer. "Uh-oh, here come city ways," said Otis, and then: "Now you want to hear the vagabond's psychology?" Shane stretched back, elbows on the floorboards of the porch, and took pursing sips while he listened to what Otis had to say. "Sam won't talk, but it's worse that he won't feel what he also doesn't say. Silence should be a sign of something felt but too deep for words. Not so in Sam. He buries the thoughts and the words, both. Try tracing a faint smile on his lip back to any laughter in his eye. Can't be done. That's Sam. His parts don't tot up. We all find signs in him, but it depends on whether you're watching his gait or his carriage, or his hands or his brow — you hate him, you love him, you seek him out, you run from him. Opinion varies on Sam. Talk about him on different days, comes out different. What is he? He hates everybody. But think of those good times you can have with him. But as soon as you see his smile, just watch, close up, it's really a sneer, isn't it? But he's not hard by nature. Something soft's in there. Yes, but when you've seen it, look out, now he's steely. He'll choose his peril, and then he'll escape it by chance. But does he escape? Chance comes back, choice comes back, I guess it's all just destiny. He'll soar beyond or sink beneath it — either will do. But, damn, he's condemned to breathe our air with us. He's an erring spirit in our world; he'd probably rather his blood flowed ice. Wait, but in his defense, he rarely says anything to hurt you. See how it goes? He'd like to remain unseen, so he says, but he has the art of fixing himself in your memory. You dwell on his few words. You ponder his mood. How does he do it? He entwines himself around your mind. You greet him once and already he's stamped there. And then he grows there. You can't get to his soul, but damn if he isn't getting to yours. Something now within you forces your attention to him. It's a trick. And now, look, Shane, it's happened

to you. You don't know him either. Is he what you'd call —
I believe your word was — gay? No, he's not gay, surely;
he's the village stud. So what is he? Lonely wanderer?
Exile? Kidnapper of Arab boys? Fugitive? In mourning for
his life? He's made you do his grieving for him. See what
I mean? There's his psychology. He's caught you in his net.
That's Sam. His spirit dares you to forget him."

"Can't be done," echoed Shane, his glass drained to the
flopping green rind of lime, which he tapped down into his
mouth for a few good chews. Then a healthy spit catapulted
it into the holly bush by the stairs.

But if Sam had caught Shane, and Emmy, and Sue Otto
(up on the hilltop late into the night reading novel upon
novel, by her chair a bag of potato chips or packet of cookies, her millside oriel spreading the yellow lamplight across
the village hall roof), if Sam had all of us, then who would
catch Sam, to pull him back inside, with his comrades,
home again? And at Thanksgiving? No one — for he would
sit in his dim granite hall, with the young man who spoke
no English, imagining it any other day. He had declined the
invitation of the Ottos, retreated from the overtures of the
Januses — no, not in his own old house, he was sorry, not
on Thanksgiving (they understood entirely), and he had
avoided Sunny and Dick Reichardt, who just might have
had it in mind to offer places to him and Khaled at their
groaning board.

So it was left for the next season to bring him back
amongst his fellows. There is a festival that can't be set
aside: if the Harvest Home draws villagers to their own
hearths, the Yuletide requires making merry in a throng.
What's more, that year the Ottos had come to the hun-

dredth Christmas atop their hill. There would be some carousing. The whole of Otis Pond — Khaled, too — was expected to become one with all. Those computing Bodmans, those antisocial Blairs, everyone . . . Jim Ezzelino was to handle the catering. His restaurant staff, from Keene, would serve that night. Otis Pond had holiday.

VIII

The hilltop house was illumined before nightfall in that earliest darkness of the year. On the northeast corner, where the driveway ascended, the music room windows already beckoned bright, but the windows of study, dining room and parlor vied with a fringe of sunset beyond the pond until, almost in an instant, the sky's light drained to a cold gray and those shiny flat panes of glass dissolved into parallelepipeds of translucent gold.

The next day was the eve of Christmas, and Christmas itself fell on a Friday; Fred Otto, thankful for another year in the black, had presented his millworkers with two additional days of paid vacation by declaring a five-day weekend. And with the Ezzelino's restaurant vans up and down the driveway all day and unknown people from Keene bustling about the Otto house, there was nothing for the villagers to prepare but themselves.

This was Joanie Voshell's busiest season, of course, but she'd shut the post office up midafternoon anyway and strolled the pond road home. At the fork, which could take her along a little gully, barely trickling now, up into the woods to her bungalow, she decided instead to cross the culvert and drop in on Otis, her neighbor on the pond side, who'd been only a stone's throw away all her life long. Both had inherited their parents' houses, both lived alone in them now. In the days of Landes, Joanie had been a regular visitor — Landes cooked, Landes played the old piano, Landes cultivated roses. Now Otis's house was surrounded by dozens of thorny bushes gone leggy; Joanie had to weave carefully along the path to avoid getting snagged. When was the last time Otis had painted his own flaking gray clapboards? Ah, there was a light in his kitchen — if one shone in his bedroom up at the eaves she'd turn home, but the lone kitchen light told her she'd be welcome.

When they'd sat awhile at the metal-top table with their tin coffee mugs (in Otis's house, crockery and glassware were kept safely in the dining room cabinet; iron, steel and tin served duty in a kitchen that had never heard of plastic or Teflon) — when they were sitting there watching the sunlight fade and their own shapes take on substance in the smudgy windowpanes, Joanie confessed she didn't know how to handle the dilemma the evening posed for her. Her friend Chris Hrudka from Keene often got called in by Jim Ezzelino for his bigger catering jobs, and sure enough she'd be at the Ottos'. "Good, I'd like to meet her finally," Otis said, brightening. "But we agreed not to acknowledge — well, maybe a hello's all right, 'don't I know you from somewhere?' — that sort of thing. It's just too delicate, Otis." "You can't introduce me to your new friend?" "This isn't like you and Landes, Otis. She's got her kids. We're being careful." "Well, point her out to me at least." "Oh, there's no mistaking Chris," Joanie said with a hoot and then, as she sustained a sip of her coffee, her eyes lit up: "See this?" She was reaching across the table to grab a green pear in its tissue paper from a box of two dozen sent from Washington State by Landes, as he'd done each Christmas for three years now. Joanie unwrapped the fruit and balanced it on her palm. "That's Chris," she said. She pinched the pear's buttocks and gave a quick kiss to its tiny head then nestled it back in the packing.

"You know, Ezzelino's has got those cornball outfits from some Robin Hood pageant their caterers wear for Christmas parties. I can just see all us clodhoppers up at the Otto house with the shrinks and profs like we belonged there and this bunch of Oldie Englishie peasants waltzing around with trays of antipasto!" "Well, Fred's heart's in the right place," said Otis. "Oh Otis," moaned Joanie suddenly, "I'm being a sourpuss. Sometimes everybody strikes me as ridiculous, that's all. No, not you. If I couldn't see your roof through the trees on days like this one, I think I'd skip off to Florida." Should she have said that? Joanie watched Otis's face for a sign, but he wasn't giving one. The prospect of her girlfriend passing her a stuffed mushroom was surely nothing to his anxiety at socializing with Sam Lara as fellow villagers, everyone cocking an ear to catch an echo of ancient rumor.

Since Landes's departure, having coffee first thing in the morning over in Joanie's little cat-filled kitchen generally launched Otis's day. She knew she should have avoided mentioning, even if only to renounce it, the notion of her skipping off anywhere. After Landes, after other less steady flames — after Sam, for that matter — no wonder Otis changed the subject now: "I wonder who'll talk to Khaled tonight," he said, seeming suddenly amused at the prospect, "or maybe he'll just wait patiently in a corner looking androgynous." "He'd make a great lesbian," said Joanie. "Yes, even that faint little trace of mustache," Otis said with a sly smile.

Joanie was getting up to go home. "What'll you wear, Otis?" "I thought perhaps doublet and hose in Lincoln green," he said, but when he leaned back in his spindly kitchen chair, he displayed blue jeans and blue-green plaid shirt and admitted, "No, what you see is all you get." "How about putting on a tie?" Joanie ventured. "I have only one tie," said Otis, "and it's reserved for funerals." But as she slipped out the door, Joanie commanded in mock grimness: "Wear it!"

Later, when they reached the Dokes' foot-of-the-hill house, for a hundred years home to the Ottos' office managers, they saw Emmy and Shane coming toward them from the plaza, hand in hand. The kids were in their church clothes, and Emmy's coat lapel bore a sprig of holly. With only a dusting of snow, the driveway was usefully crunchy for their ascent. Up there shone the music room, its arching rafters looped with evergreen garlands, candles in the chandelier. With every step, there was more to see: a few guests' heads, then shoulders, the curving black lid of the grand piano agape, champagne sparkling in goblets at smiling lips, an occasional anonymous green forester circulating with a tray, and now the tootle of a soprano recorder and the bang and rattle of tambourines.

"This is going to be something else," Shane told Emmy.

"Either of you ever been up here before?" Joanie wondered. "Me? Never," said Shane. "I think maybe when I was a baby," Emmy said. "Gee, and I zip up here every morning," said Joanie, "but can't say I ever get past the kitchen — " "What about for Gwen Otto's wedding?" Otis reminded her, but Joanie confessed she'd been too stoned to register on the house what with one of Gwen's college crowd liberally passing the pipe. Shane shook his head at all this. "My dad always said the kids Aunt Rosemarie's age were the wild ones in town." "Well, certainly no one ever caught Bill Troyer with *his* pants down," said Joanie. "And he said it was only Sam Lara that made the others of you look good by comparison." "Is Sam going to be here tonight?" Emmy wanted to know.

"There!" said Otis. He pointed at the closest window, now only the driveway's width away. A tall figure had crossed before them and stood now with one hand on the open piano's lower lip steadying his glass, watching bubbles rise up at him. He seemed to smile — Sam Lara smiling? — and from that distance, through the window, his eyes and brow seemed to smile, too. He raised his head. Sunny Reichardt was fluttering over to him, Dick by her side.

At the east door, the green strangers efficiently swept up the kids' overcoats, then Joanie's jacket and Otis's gloves and thick wool scarf — when he'd unwound it, Joanie was startled to see he'd worn his tie. It was darkest blue, almost black, with diagonal threads of gold barely distinguishable. She remembered it as one of the ties Landes used to wear to his county job in Keene.

Emmy and Shane were already at the music room door

receiving champagne from Friar Tuck. Otis and Joanie made their way into the parlor, instead. The fire was blazing nicely even without Otis's tending. And here came the Januses, Pat with green bow tie, Susan in floor-length skirt of red and gold; they looked like Grams and Gramps in a Christmas card. We'll abandon Otis and Joanie to them; the conversation will contain nothing we haven't already heard. But across the hall, drawn by toot-peep and thump-rattle-thump, we're more likely to find something new afoot.

Kathee Thompson from the store had glommed onto her contemporaries as soon as they stepped into the music room. "Emmy, see that man Mac Rhodes is chewing the ear off of? That's Jim Ezzelino from Keene." Shane leaned in to hear what the girls were whispering. "See him keep looking over at Sam Lara?" Of course, Kathee had been watching Sam herself and, sensitive to subtle eye movements, had noticed she wasn't the only one. Sam was now leaning against the piano, arms folded across his black sweater; he'd finished his champagne and gazed out through the crowd. Sunny and Dick were cavorting pseudomedievally to pipe and tabor; the green foresters (yes, one *was* quite bottom heavy) were doing their bit by tapping a tray or tinking an empty glass. It was Franklin, the Otto son, and his wife Sandy providing the music; they lived in an Early Music commune down in Massachusetts and seemed to visit home only when Dad asked them to perform.

Sam would ill brook the scrutiny of this Jim Ezzelino, if he noticed it, but he hadn't yet. Large expansive Mac Rhodes, owner of the village store and master of the interminable anecdote, was oblivious to both the ballet and Ezzelino's drifting eye; Mac's experience of human beings, no doubt, had been that they tended to drift into the distance during social intercourse. Ezzelino was cautiously masking his inspection of Sam with a proprietary concern for overseeing his band of serving folk. He was careful, himself, not to appear of their number; dressed circa 1992, a guest at the Christmas party of a fellow member of the Chamber of Commerce, he was rather more Sheriff of Nottingham than Robin Hood. Indeed, there was a Robin in the study, dispensing the hard stuff at a makeshift minibar, and that's where Ezzelino had been — with Otto and Doke and some computer genius named Bodman (wasn't it?) and Gault from the court and Murray from the bank, but then that annoying new Unitarian minister woman had come in and he'd fled, only to be trapped by Rhodes, more annoying still — and who *was* that tall man leaning against the piano? So damn familiar, but not from here, not from here . . .

It has to happen, when mutually random glances cast themselves about a room, that at last they encounter each other, and when these two did it was in mute amazement. Unfathomable emotion gathered in Lara's now steadied gaze, distrusting that which the man in the stylish dark suit threw back at him; Ezzelino's eyes, fixed and stern, flashed across the room some wild tale in a code Kathee and Emmy and Shane couldn't begin to decipher. "It's him," said Ezzelino, not imagining Rhodes would stop his droning. But, anxious for any sort of interactive counterpoint, the store owner leaned even closer toward him and said, eagerly, "It's who?"

Fred and Carol Otto had come to the doorway to watch the dancing, but their son and daughter-in-law were just winding up their sarabande or galliard or whatever it was, and in that second between cadence and applause, Mac Rhodes's "It's who?" boomed forth like two concluding drumbeats. The applause faltered as soon as it began; something else was about to occur. Sam didn't move, his aspect didn't change. The surprise that had sprung across his face had subsided; his eyes showed nothing now, though Jim Ezzelino still glared and repeated, ostensibly to Mac but, as the room fell quiet, with a sneer meant for all to assess: "It's him." And then in the dead silence: "How did he ever get out of there? What's he doing here in Otis Pond?"

Fred Otto stepped forward, the embryonic Italian restaurant project quivering in his imagination's womb. The company was now stepping back, and the polished parquet shone bare between Fred and Jim and Sam. But before Fred could explain that this was the man he'd been telling Jim about, the one with the mill downstream, that beautiful old granite mill, the future Trattoria-on-the-Quidnapunxet, or Ezzelino's-in-the-Woods, or — Sam stepped forward himself and with a collected look and mild firmness in his voice, nothing petulant or overbold, said: "My name is Lara. When I know who you are, I'll answer your questions."

"You'll answer my questions!" Ezzelino scoffed. "You better think if there isn't a question you already have to answer in your own heart every day of your damn life! All the time in the world isn't going to let you forget what I know about you. You want to know who I am?"

Lara — he didn't seem Sam at that moment but Lara again, the notorious youth, grown haggard gray but still subject of fearful whispers, speculative gasps — Lara looked over at this man who questioned him. His eyes grew, searching slowly, but, finding in Ezzelino no trace he recognized or chose to recognize, he said nothing. With that dubious look that, in the teenage Lara, had marked a half contempt for whatever came his way, he turned to the door to pass the trembling Ottos.

Ezzelino, who got there as quickly, thrust out his arm. "You'd better answer me, Lara. Mr. Otto's going to want to know. No, Fred, listen, if I'm out of line, let him say so. He's pulled some wool over your eyes. And you were proposing a business partnership with this man?" The hallway was as jam-packed as the room, even Robin Hood had left his bottles and hopped on Friar Tuck's shoulders under the mistletoe-bedecked chandelier so he could see over the clustered heads to the music room door. The host was sputtering: "But, but . . ." and then the hostess began to say, "It's Christmas, please," but still the accuser pressed his case. "Answer me one simple thing. Aren't you the one? The one who did — " "Whatever I am," said Lara's voice, muffled by the crush of people but cold and clear as new ice, "whatever I am, I'm not hearing it from you. You've got your crowd. Tell them. But I'll thank Mr. Otto now for inviting me and — " "Wait a minute, you both," said Fred, "this is our party!" His face was reddening even to the whites of his eyes, and his collar looked too tight, his jaw shaky. "Please, this is for the village. Jim, I promise you, Sam will come up tomorrow, we'll meet then just the three of us, talk it out. I know Sam, even though he's been away so long. He'll keep his word. That's my pledge. You'll both have it out privately tomorrow here with me. But this is our party. Let's not spoil the general mirth. We've been having a fine time. Your food's splendid, Jim, and we've hardly even begun eating it. They're just opening up the dining room now. Wait till you all see what Ezzelino's has cooked for us. Sandy, sing, please. Franklin, some caroling? Lead us into the dining room?" The Otto daughter-in-law tapped her tambourine and shook it over her head while her voice soared embarrassingly into "God rest ye merry, gentlemen" as her husband piped a descant. No one wanted to move to let them through till Chris Hrudka, holding her empty tray up like a shield, cleared a path.

"Tomorrow," said Jim Ezzelino as the guests began to shuffle by him, "all right. But what's this Lara say?" Sunny and Dick, the Tarnoff-Rices, Gwen Otto and her straggle-haired doped-up husband Tim, Ann Doke holding on to Peter, Dorothy Paulson, Mrs. Collins — all tried to catch a glimpse into Sam's soul as they passed. He seemed sunk in deep abstraction; that he noticed no one and met no one's eyes bespoke a memory only too profound. "All right, tomorrow." All he said. No anger flashed in his face. Something fixed in his low tones showed unknown but resolved determination. He bowed his head slightly as he stepped around Ezzelino then met the latter's frown with one of his disconnected smiles. It wasn't a smile of happiness nor of pride struggling to curb wrath; it was the smile of a man sure in his own heart of all he could ever manage to do or endure. Did it reveal the goodness in him and spell peace or was it a sign of guilt grown old, of desperate hardihood?

The first time you had to confront that look of Sam's, it

shattered something in you. However much you usually trusted what you saw, what you heard, suddenly you didn't. You realized, in a glance, that only this man's deeds could tell you what you had to know, that his deeds alone would teach you the truth that, to learn, would wring your unpracticed heart.

IX

He seized his black cape from a man in Lincoln green and spoke a strange word, like a cough transforming itself in one breath to a song, and there Khaled was, by his side, having slipped through the crowd against its current. The attachment was secure. For Sam Lara he'd already given up his sunnier clime where with stars the nights, too, were brighter. He was always sedate, even amid these raucous Yankees at their feast. He'd stood in the parlor by the fire, appreciating the blaze through the thin white muslin of his trousers. Earlier, a chatty retired couple had done all they could to draw him out. "How are you liking it here in New Hampshire?" the husband had asked. "Oh, Pat, he's already quite at home, you can tell," said the wife, and then she'd added in overly distinct syllables: "We welcome you to Otis Pond." Khaled had smiled and nodded and uttered a thank you as he took a handful of cashew nuts from the bowl the wife was holding out to him. "Do you understand English?" asked the husband, eyes twinkling with helpfulness. "He's picked up quite a lot I'll bet," said the wife. Khaled nodded, or did he shake his head? — a little of each. She went on: "I'm sure Sam's been teaching him. Sam's so bookish." "Sam Lara," Khaled affirmed. What a relief to the lady and gentleman: they were communicating with the Arab. "I hear he's fixing up the old mill nicely — " "Well, but I think it's just a temporary job, Pat. Who knows what he has in mind eventually? We were talking about him, Khaled, with the postmistress and our housepainter over there . . ." "We're somewhat new in town ourselves, you see, but Susan's already got her finger on the pulse of the village. Villages are remarkable institutions. And getting scarcer . . ." And so the trialogue went, until such time as Khaled was set free by the commotion across the hall.

As silent as the man he served, he embodied a slow-moving, closemouthed faithfulness contrary to the expected wayward habits of his young years and menial station. Only when, from Sam's lips, he heard again the accents of his native land did his step become fleet, his own voice clear in response, though still gibberish to local ears. No doubt, Sam's Arabic (if Arabic it was) woke absent echoes in his soul: voices of childhood comrades, his kin, his own parents, all lost now, abjured for just one friend — his all. The whole earth now disclosed for him no other guide; no wonder he was rarely out of Sam's hailing.

From across the parlor, watching him bespangled by fire-light in the midst of dull conversation, you might imagine Khaled was sorrowing. His brow delicately darkened but not marred by desert sun, and his cheek with its unbidden blush (not so much the healthy hue of a delighted heart as a more hectic tint, a sign of feverish secret cares burning within), and then the wild sparkle of his eye lighted as if

with electric thought but always tempered by the fringe of
his long lash — these all still showed less of sorrow, really,
than of pride. If he grieved it was a grief he would let no
one share, not even (it seemed) Sam.

It had been noted in Otis Pond that he wasn't inclined
toward any kind of sport; he always passed by the after-
work soccer dribblers on the plaza, which disappointed
their hopes of picking up a little third-world finesse; surely,
lithe as he was, Khaled might have had a thing or two to
show these New Englanders who hadn't yet got the game
in their bones. But Khaled would slope apologetically along
the mill wall and escape into the store to buy fixings for
Sam's supper. You never saw him jog up the road or swing
from a tree limb (like Shane Troyer); even sober Otis Cable
seemed a more vibrant athlete than this young man from
Qatar, or wherever he really came from. If you asked Khaled
something, his answer (as the Januses had found) would be
most brief — a yes, a no, usually unvoiced, and he never
asked a question back, so no one could determine how
much he'd understood. Kathee Thompson was convinced
he caught on to everything; she'd heard him chuckling over
the Akbar and Jeff cartoon book he took three days making
up his mind to purchase. But Ann Doke, who'd quizzed
him in the library when he brought back the overdue *Lusiads* for Sam, was sure he couldn't tell our alphabet from
mere scrawl, and when she'd tried to commiserate with
him on cold weather (muffled as he was in his Eskimo
suit), he hadn't caught her meaning; she'd tried enacting
a shivering fit, but he just wriggled about inside the parka
as if he thought she was teaching him a jolly new American
dance. On sunnier days, you might see him swathed in that

white padding, his boots dangling over the dam, sadly watching the icy cascade, but you saw little evidence of that pleasure Ed Forgan had been so privileged to glimpse when first he saw Khaled awestruck among the falling leaves. To most eyes, he remained a young man who had taken from nature only the bitter boon of his birth; you had to look much closer, into that dark face, to see that the one thing he loved, Samuel Lara, now encompassed all.

In silent attendance, Khaled could fulfill a wish of Sam's before Sam's tongue expressed it. Still, there was a haughtiness in all Khaled did: it was only in the mere act that he seemed to obey; in its manner, he commanded. His zeal was nothing servile, as if he always served less Sam's desire than his own. He opened for Sam the jeep's passenger door, closed it firmly and like a careful sheepdog safely steered his shepherd home. There, he'd turn up the lamp beside that frightful skull, so Sam might peruse *The Idylls of the King* in better light; and then he'd bar the door at midnight, fold back the quilts, and warm the bottom sheet with embers from the stove in a copper pan.

Most villagers had avoided him at the Ottos' Christmas, not because they wouldn't have liked to know more of him but because his reserve exuded no perceptible sympathy. Language was not the sole barrier; indeed, many a villager greeted another and joked and strolled on with but a monosyllable and a wink in the eye. But something in Khaled's eyes denoted a higher birth than theirs and better days than these; vulgar toil was not for him, and his hands might have been judged feminine if there hadn't been something else (beyond his masculine garb), something in his gaze more wild and high than a woman's, some latent fierceness derived from his fiery desert birthplace and quite unsuited to his spare and tender frame in our northern woodlands. In short, in his few words he might have seemed a gentle fellow, but his aspect was unsettling and made villagers stand back from him. Peter Doke, in a whimsical mood, imagined him a terrorist; it would be just like Sam to plant a Palestinian assassin amongst us — what better way for Sam now to avenge the tribulations of his youth? "They have profiles, the airport security, the customs officials, they know what to look out for," Peter said. "I bet this Khaled's a perfect fit!"

Something funny about that name, too. Peter and Ann, Otis, Joanie and Ed, too, one day at lunch discovered how each of them had, on one occasion or another, addressed the foreigner by name, and the young man had seemed not to hear, as if his own name were unfamiliar, did not belong to him. It couldn't have been their mispronouncing of it; whom else could they have meant? But only on their second or third try, as if he'd just remembered he was now called Khaled, he'd smiled and returned the greeting. "He's got another name back in Libya, it's obvious," said Peter, "and probably it's Saddam!" "Sodomite, more likely," said Ed with a quick jab at Otis's rib cage. "Where'd you learn such a long word, Ed?" quipped unruffled Otis.

But Sam himself never lapsed in calling him Khaled, and Khaled never failed to turn his head when that name came from Sam's lips. Then ear, eye and heart would all awake. So there it was, perhaps: the rest of them kept back from him because they knew Khaled's soul was only for Sam Lara; why should they bother to try to draw him over to themselves?

Now, when the strife had suddenly commenced in the Ottos' music room and the press of the crowd had prevented him from immediately reaching Lara's side, Khaled's color came and went — lip of ashes, cheek of flame, sickening iciness on his damp forehead and his thought (at once shrinking from the occurrence and yet dreaming and daring and executing it all before the thoughts were half aware) now sealed his lips and sent the agonies up to crease his brow. He found himself staring at the trim back of Jim Ezzelino's head, clipped close at the ears, shaved high on the neck, a military head, battle ready. Nudging closer, straining on tiptoe, Khaled caught the slight bowing of Sam Lara's head as he stepped around his adversary and then that sidelong smile, disconnected at its corners from cheek, from eye, but a sign that Khaled alone could read of something buried terrifyingly deep. Khaled sprang after him through the clot of guests. At the door, Sam's long and dark shadow, as he whirled his cape up and around himself, was relieving the glare of the Christmas lights strung outside along the porte cochere; Khaled was instantly there to hand him his gloves, and, in a moment, both were gone.

All within the house seemed left suddenly alone. They had been fixing their eyes on Lara's mien, attempting to assess it, but now a mix of all the old feelings rushed at them: this returned rebel with his aloof companion, invaders of their small quiet world, better without them — and yet how stunningly calmly Sam had borne the insult, how marvelous he still was, proud as ever. There must be some awful tale to be told, some dark dream — the worst is always nearest the truth.

Jim Ezzelino was, of course, still present, the one person

with no need to guess: apparently, he knew the tale. But Fred Otto, as host, as employer, as benefactor, had skillfully postponed the telling; no villager now would dare be so impolite as to try to wheedle further information out of Mr. Ezzelino.

As promised, the dining table was piled high, with such food as was seldom tasted in Otis Pond: spicy and sweet sausages, Parmesan eggplant and garlic cloves steamed whole, chicken pieces drenched in marsala, bubbling cheeses, pickled cauliflower, snails and squid and tart anchovies and quantities of Sue Otto's favorite *tiramisù*, the "pull-me-up" she claimed she needed to combat her Christmas blues. (She'd put on twenty pounds since Thanksgiving and seemed bent on doubling that by New Year's.)

Jim Ezzelino accepted all compliments, when Fred and Carol refused them, and with a somewhat imperious air watched the frenzied feeders, their red and green plastic plates and napkins and their picnic forks and tumblers of Chianti and Rhine wine all precarious as they ate and drank and snuck back in line for more, wishing they all had three hands. Only Melvin Tarnoff-Rice approached the caterer confidentially, stabbing a meatball while balancing the rest in his large fingers. "I wish I could be up here tomorrow," the doctor said, knowingly, though surely he knew nothing at all. "Perhaps I was in error," he admitted, "when I diagnosed Mr. Lara — not to his face, mind you — as a forgivable sort of prodigal son. His legendary status hereabouts has seemed out of all proportion to me. But perhaps you're about to prove me wrong." One piercing psychoanalytic glare and off he went, nibbling calamari in the direction of the desserts.

When at last the crowd had gone, when the revelers were

at rest and the courteous hosts had crept to their accustomed bed, Ezzelino and his merry men (and women) labored on awhile. Then the vans from Keene pulled round the house to the lower door, and the crew was ready with great plastic bags of undegradable refuse, with aluminum trays caked with dried cheeses and rubberized pasta or slippery with tomato gravy, ready also with cases of clanking empty wine bottles (they had gustily polished off whatever dribs remained), with cartons containing the caps and jerkins and tights and felt boots they'd doffed in relief, riotously reverting to their late-twentieth-century selves and in the process, briefly, half nude and lusty, chasing each other off into the recesses of the Otto basement, Robin and Marian and Tuck and all — they were ready, finally, with their own bundled-up selves piling tightly into the cabs of the vans. Who's going in which? Which van's going past the new mall? Where did Chris go? And the boss shook every hand and wished them all Buon Natale — and see you tomorrow at three to get the bank's gala ready — and then he ducked into his little Alfa Romeo (license plate MANGIA, with the state's unavoidable Live Free or Die) which he'd parked on the lip of the hill to leave just enough room for his fleet to pass. He waved them all by, and then, after the way had time to clear and he'd made an enticing offer to a part-time Otto family retainer over there locking up the back door — "I could give you a lift, or we could maybe . . ." followed by a gesture that might mean any number of things — he sped off with his last-minute passenger at an unrecommended speed through two darkened portes cocheres, down the precipitous driveway, and then (with a screech) took a sharp right toward the plaza, to the

bridge ("YOU'RE LEAVING OTIS POND . . .") And then the
county road over the ridge to the post road, at last, where
he could let it out all the way.

Back in the village, sweet forgetfulness had descended.
Who back there could ever have been coaxed drunkenly
out on the dark roads of the world beyond? No, they rested
in night's sepulcher, the universal home, glad to heave unconscious breath awhile. There would be time enough,
when they woke, to wrestle again with their dread.

❀   ❀   ❀

I shall wait a page or two before beginning what I might consider my second canto. I have to remind myself, for a moment, of me. In this little library, each afternoon, I write these pages with me at a remove, forgetting myself almost, as I was, as I am, and then off I totter home, at three score and ten a relic in this village of unfamiliar and unfriendly white folk. Oh, that's just how I think of them. I'm ostensibly white, too, but not like these refugees from the collapsing metropolises. They're as strange to me as the three Blairs, those early transplants who never bothered to decline Fred and Carol Otto's invitation but simply didn't show up. Now they're all like that here. The Tarnoff-Rices, Bodmans and Januses had been, it turns out, the best of them, still sufficiently in the minority to look upon us natives with respect. But the psychoanalysts soon found a classier place over in Peterborough, the Bodmans were suddenly transferred to San Jose and Susan Janus (once Professor Pat had died) followed that overbearing son of hers to South Carolina. Those Blairs, however, with their gothic taste in library books, their closed windowshades, their car alarms and low hat brims, stayed grimly on to inspire a society of their own ilk, marked by as much indifference to one another as to us. Apparently, they'd been so engulfed by mistrust in their cities, here they craved only to be left undisturbed. Nowadays, when I emerge from the library onto the warm windy plaza (it's September, summer struggles to persist) and see a blank face passing silently from its office in the old Otto Mill to its dwelling out the pond road, I wait till it (man, woman) has vanished. Perhaps it knows others of its tribe, but it doesn't know me.

There are a few of us left. Barrett Troyer, not so far from fifty now himself, has lived with me for twenty years nearly, but his brother Shane has been gone awhile, and Emmy too, each sadly in a separate direction. Sunny and Dick do stumble to the plaza occasionally from their retirement apartment (they were the last of us to get in); the Dokes are still over in Keene. We hang on. Joanie and Chris write now and again from what sounds to me like their hellhole in Florida. Ed Forgan's been dead for some years. Attended still by ancient Judy, Sue Otto sits in her hilltop house, enormously fat, her taste in books in serious decline. She'll read anything that comes into the library, this dumping ground for "old" books — look, there's the complete hardbound uniform edition of Stephen King (I've found out who he was) donated, I believe, by the Blairs, who don't need the actual books now they're so easily accessible electronically. By the millennium, Mrs. Collins's successor, a certain Leota Colburn, had weeded out most of the Otto collection trying to appeal to the more contemporary reader, as she put it. I, the implicated anachronism, picked up the weekly carton of rejects before Ed Forgan's truck

could spirit it away and staggered home with it. Barrett's
a slowish reader, but he's still finding things he likes, and
they do help insulate a room, he admits, shelved tight along
the northern exposure. This Leota Colburn, hardened by
years teaching sixth grade in cities, likes in her retirement
nothing more than cuddling up with good old-fashioned
Danielle Steel or Harold Robbins — takes her back to her
youth. She reprieved certain items of the original collection, but only if they had handsome spines; a rip or a crack
might disqualify Volume Two, say, of a three-part novel,
which made a mess of Trollope and Dickens, but from this
side of the room, far enough to distinguish no titles, those
few shelves of "classics" look beautiful, framing the south
window bright with the afternoon sun.

What the current librarian never knew, what Sue Otto
has forgotten, what I cling to in my old age is that those
books still speak in their clear responsive tongues: responsive, I'll say it again — they speak back to us. Take a tale
by Lord Byron — as I've promised, this volume of mine
will succeed his on that shelf over there. Mightn't I recognize the secrets of my own life embedded in one of those
high romantic tales? Can't I transform myself in imagination — no, not me, but my various parts, my essences —
into the forces thrashing at each other in one or another
old poem? Must we see ourselves in everything only drear-
ily as we are now? Or mightn't the fury of a love betrayed,
the ardor of faithful companionship, an avenger's passion,
a great man's fall, the demise of a fortune, the ecstasy of
nature in all its rustling beauty — mightn't these things
arouse our souls in any age?

But it's not the age, actually; look at these "gothics"

here by my chair, the ones with lumpy paper covers, copy-
right — hmm — 1992, well-thumbed, one avid reader more
and they'll go poof! No, it's the language. It's become too
difficult. Even I, as I write now, write a different language
from theirs out there, a language difficult twenty-odd years
ago, a language I began learning at the dawn of the atomic
age when it was already only a moldering encrustation
about the spoken word. And now it might as well have
been written two hundred years back for all my neighbors
know; it's as dead as the language of the Pennacooks. I
confine my public utterances to a nope and a yep, a nod,
an ambiguous wink. I seldom speak to anyone on the plaza,
and no one approaches me. I still have a few odd tasks I
perform about town; Barrett (who comprehends the household monitor programs) keeps rather busier — he's the Otis
Cable of the day. And they'll ask him questions about old
times, which they'd never dare ask me. They don't know
if I'm his lover or his father, not that it matters much to
them. We're the codgers, the cranky oldster and the not-
so-cranky younger one, but still sort of cranky, cranky
enough, humorous, quaint, queer.

Is this the familiar song of the generations? Do we all —
will even they — come eventually to this, this loss of our
voices? Do we all, as Barrett Troyer used to tell his little
brother Shane, see for ourselves someday? I suppose, but
why may I look back two centuries and feel still at home,
while they cannot look back two decades? Those Blairs, in
their first years here — such brave pioneers in primitive
circumstances! — had no idea the real village was gasping
its last in a drama totally unwitnessed, irrelevant, not
worth noting, for all their love of scary stories. But for me,

those years! Landes had left, Barrett and I had not yet found the way to each other and my mournful imagination — lost, groping, hopeless — could easily be caught up in a wild tale of a beloved's return, of an unforgiven insult reiterated, of the thwarting of a terrible revelation, of a haunting embodiment of devotion even unto death. How it spun out inside me a confused web of my own agony, how I grappled with it, entangled, cocooned, smothered. O reading! You are as much the wise old woman in the woods at night as she I encountered in younger days under the moon in autumn. I still feel her spirit now, not often, but enough to keep me here, she, like you, the emblem of an unspoken language — her Pennacook, your Byronic English. Otis Pond still embraces this remnant of a library, still shines in moonlight outside my attic window where I sleep with my younger love, and she hovers out there, like you — two ghosts over the water. I must take a midnight walk to the hillock of the graveyard tonight, stretch out on the yellowing grass, lean against a gravestone by a birch tree, wait for the presence to speak again: Old man, listen. Listen to the tale of these hills, this little valley, this silvery flat water. (No one yet has dared wreck the old dam with dynamite!) Keep it all in your heart. Do not ever leave here. Take my place for me.

I

Light woke up the world, and we'd begun again. Vapors were curling around the hills, and in the distance to the east the stormy forehead of Monadnock unveiled to the ever slightly earlier returning sun. One more day now swelled our past; each of our last days was now one nearer. But for Nature, as every day, it was just another birth. Into the sickening air of a waning century, she bounded forth, mighty as ever. What was the millennium to her? Bad winds and drought, freak April snows, steamier summers, rising instances of skin cancer, branches yellowed, filthy water — these were our poor cares, not hers. She comprised it all — stain, acid, stench and blight. Watch her now, we told ourselves, watch her because we'll go long before she does. She doesn't die off like a human language; she adjusts. Perhaps she even relishes her poisonous new colorations; she's been poisonous before. Do earth and sky weep for us? Does leaf fall? Gale breathe? The worms will still have something to do, long past our time.

It was the morning of the eve of Christmas, approaching

noon. Otis Cable had been at the Ottos' helping put things back in place. Carol directed him in repositioning the chairs and stacking plates and bowls, and then one more scrub-down was required before contending with her own family's party that night. Judy was again in glad possession of her kitchen, but Fred Otto lurked nervously upstairs in his study. No exact time had been set, he realized, for the confrontation, but surely they'd come soon, not to dampen the holiday unduly. He'd called the Casa Ezzelino, but no one yet had seen the boss that morning; Fred would send Otis Cable for phoneless Sam if he didn't show up soon. Should he pour himself a sherry to calm down? Otis, who'd surely witnessed the contretemps, seemed strangely calm that morning, almost shrugging it off where Fred expected him to commiserate nervously. But Carol was worried, so was Sue, for indeed some awful depth had been sounded and the plumb line was about to be pulled back up, here in Fred's study. Whatever was down there, deep in Sam, might be more than Fred cared to uncover; it was a more appealing prospect having the wanderer reveal, in his own good time, his quaint tales of foreign custom, startling adventure, lucky escapes and a grateful return home. Such accounting put the world back together; it didn't sunder it as Jim seemed bent on doing. What did Fred know about Jim, actually? A single fellow, obviously of Italian descent, learned his trade abroad — in a Swiss hotel, wasn't that it? As astute at business as in the culinary arts. A bit humorless. But reasonable dealing with him on the Chamber of Commerce . . .

Fred sat deep in his soft leather chair and stared out at the northern hill beyond the pond, its pines freshly dusted white late last night, and farther to the higher slopes that funneled small Quidnapunxets into one. A sip of sherry, now, but it didn't still the tremor in his heart. Oh! He sensed Otis in the doorway behind him and turned. He's here? Who? Ah, it's Sam.

The brother miller entered, black cape over forearm, self-confiding, with a coldly patient air. "Have a seat." Fred was awkward. The rules of friendly visits couldn't apply here. Sam Lara sank into the chair opposite, a third plainly empty between them. "Can Otis get you anything?" "Oh no," said Sam, "but Otis — " The handyman was hesitating at the door. "And Fred — " Sam had to wait and think, to put it as precisely as he could, to both of them, not as to servant and master but to his two fellow villagers, men he'd grown up with, men who knew him. In a soft voice: "I'm only here because of you. Both of you, in fact." Otis's stare grew piercing, and Sam looked away, to the cabinet of carved oak, brought from the Rhineland by the first Otto, its open door displaying the disparate bottles, squat and tall, some still sealed up with wax, others hoarding their last drops. Sam began muttering: "Why should I have to hear from this Ezzelino character? I've been around the world a couple of times. Do you know how many madmen there are in it? He says he knew me in — well, I never let him say, did I? So why should I hear it today either? I've heard what people had to say about me all my life. As if they knew a thing. You didn't know much, Fred. But you practically booted me out thirty years ago — good to get away, just what you need, fresh start, new battles." "Oh Christ, Sam, I didn't boot you out!" Fred couldn't help but say. "We walked, we talked, I listened, I tried to give you encouragement for whatever it was you wanted to do."

But Sam shook his shaggy head and sank deeper into the soft dark leather. "Same with you, Otis," he said in a still lower mutter. "You never knew what you did to me any more than I knew what I'd done to you." "Now, Sam," said Fred, sitting forward, edgy, a quaver in his voice, "this isn't a time to trouble Otis. This has to do with Jim Ezzelino." Sam burst out with "So where the hell is he, Fred? You get me up here, with you acting like a judge. I'm here to listen to a damn liar. But here I am anyway, waiting."

"I'll vouch for Jim's coming. He never missed a board meeting. He was always sitting at the table before the others of us got there. Damn, I should've set a time last night. I've called, left a message. He's got the bank gala this evening, so he has to be here soon." Otis was making a move, perhaps to go put in another call, but Sam caught him. "Hey, Otis, this guy's a forfeit, isn't he? Admit it then. He was probably drunk. You two just want to find out what he had to say. Hell, he's forgotten it now he's sober, but you two are still out vulturing. What do you suppose it was? Rape or murder, or something worse?"

Fred Otto had just stood up, but what did Sam care that he himself was hunkering low and these two old friends of his now loomed so tall over him? Sam Lara was always a croucher, ready to spring loose, to feint, to bound. Why argue at eye level with mere men and their fair fights? Fool them, muddle them up, lead them off the scent, fight like animal not man. When least expected, hold knife to throat. Dodge, avoid, fade, lunge. "I pledged Jim would be here," Fred was saying, which only made Sam bark out a rude laugh. But Fred kept on, his hands twitching by his sides: "Sam, I want to resolve it, we want to leave this room with it resolved. Last night I only wanted to keep up the festiv-

ities or I would've resolved it right then." "The hell you
would've!" snarled Sam, coiling to spring. His brow had
grown almost to blackness. "Forfeit!" he suddenly bel-
lowed. How better to deal with these people than by appealing to their technicalities? Time out. Rematch. Forfeit.
Look at Fred Otto's fat flesh under his collar button, his
pulsing soft throat, veins, poor frantic blood —

But before Sam had begun to raise himself from the chair,
to walk out down the hall under the forlorn mistletoe on
the chandelier and keep his silence on the subject ever
more, Fred Otto took a dizzy step to one side, grabbed at
the back of his chair — no, it wasn't his heart at all, it was
something altogether unexpected, a kind of imbalance —
his inner ear, it felt like. He was suddenly hearing odd
buzzings, as though one ear (the left one) was emptying
out and the other filling up, his whole head awash. And
then a spinning wave hurtled to a depth and both ears
emptied out, plummeting down his throat leaving nothing
in the head at all. Otis was at his side, steadying him. Sam
was, at last, standing. Fred's eyes glimpsed the unfolding
cape, like a veil of blackness swirling out at him. His eyes
flinched, the contents of his ears were rushing back up his
gullet, expanding, filling him with roaring sound, and then
again the sloshing from side to side, empty then brimming,
and he couldn't stand.

For Otis it was just a matter of lowering him carefully
into the chair again. The turmoil wasn't visible; Fred had
only gone paler and vacant in his stare and needed to sit,
to stretch out perhaps, feet up on the hassock Otis now
retrieved from a corner. Sam was at the door, glaring as if
he loathed the paltriness of this collapse. Why no heart

attack, no stroke? What miserable fainting spell was going on over there? And Otis Cable kneeling there beside. . .

Sam looked quickly past Otis's wide black eyes, cast his own out beyond the window to the pine-forested hillsides to north and west, then fixed on that shady declivity between them, where the Upper Quidnapunxet was rushing pondward between snowy banks. But something was still down there, in the room, out of his eyes' range near the purple and crimson Oriental, two abject forms, shadows from the past, one kneeling ministering friend, the other friend in need. Sam didn't like to think about history. After all, it was gone.

Now, Otis was reaching for the phone on Fred's desk, dialing the Tarnoff-Rices. Melvin was the M.D. sort of analyst and, on his days off up here, since old Steve Henrikson's retirement the sole doctor in the village; he'd be the best judge. In haughty silence, Sam was striding purposefully from the room. While Patty (merely Ph.D.) was yelling for her husband, Otis heard Sam's jeep backing up with a lurch, then whirring off down the hill.

The doctors, both of them, pulled up in their Scirocco in hardly another minute. Soon Franklin Otto and his lackadaisical brother-in-law Tim were helping Otis and Mel carry the invalid to the couch in the parlor, where he could lie flat; they didn't want to dizzy him further on the stairs. It sounded like a species of vertigo to Mel. Faintly, Fred confessed he'd had similar, if milder, attacks before. Don't talk, Fred; don't ask him questions, anyone, not just now. Let him stay still, eyes closed, hearing the peaceful crackle of the fire, feeling the sunlight streaming in the south windows. And if he raises an eyelid, let him gaze at how the

Christmas tree shelters stacks of cheerful presents for the whole family, home together, safe on their hilltop in their village by their pond in their valley.

Otis descended to the kitchen, where Judy Nelson was stuffing the turkey. After recounting the drama of the hour, he pulled up a stool and picked over the garlicky, mushroomy bottom of the stuffing pan. Then Judy, thick arms and greasy fingers, red in the face as ever, wheezed out the next question: "So where was he?" "Who?" "Who? Lord, Otis, who else?" "Maybe he's still on his way," said Otis, who did know something of the caterer's late night out but nothing he could tell his mother's old pal Judy, nothing he could tell Fred Otto or anyone else.

The bank gala had to proceed that evening with no boss to oversee the spread. Ezzelino hadn't spent the night at his apartment above the restaurant or at his cabin up the mountain road. His car wasn't anywhere. There was no track in the snow to his garage in town and only undinted white on the lane to his cabin.

Christmas went by, and all that could be discovered — by the police, by his employees, by what little family he had in this country — was the complete absence of Jim Ezzelino. His Alfa Romeo had been seen nowhere on the highways. Nothing in his effects revealed a sign of trouble, except perhaps to provincial minds that looked cockeyed at his collection of videotapes. It was relatively wholesome stuff, or so a sympathetic state trooper concluded having viewed most of it in search of "behavior patterns" — hours and hours of smooth-bodied muscular young men rutting about, apparently delighted to be displaying themselves thus.

However, on occasions in the past, it seemed the Alfa had been spotted in a certain rest area down where the Quidnapunxet flows under the post road, where in sunny spring a young family might assemble at a creaky picnic table by the water's edge to unwrap the Whoppers they'd grabbed fast at the mall, to experience the tingle of diet soda popping on their lips like bitter kisses in the fresh air, to glory in the budding forsythia, the deep greening of mosses, the ferns shooting forth. But in the days between that Christmas and the new year, only deeper and deeper snow could tell the tale the riverbank knew. No bare branch had snagged a shred of cloth, no gout of blood had dripped on dead leaf, no struggle had defaced the frozen grass poking from the snow by the parking lot or tossed up the gravel. No print of convulsing finger was to be iden- tified on trash barrel or granite boulder (where the icy river had flung marvelous crystal webs). The Italian sports car was gone. The man was gone. Only doubting hope was left and a strange suspicion that whispered Lara's name.

II

Sharon, the wiser of her cats, had leapt into Joanie's lap. Now she rocked the two of them, a slow steady rocking that the cat expected and appreciated and that put Joanie in a meditative mood, not thinking anything out, but welcoming thoughts as they passed. Her guests — Sunny and Dick and, of course, Otis — would appear shortly. Supper was simmering, the kitchen table set.

Joanie's bungalow was nestled into the hillside on a plane with the ridgepole of the Cable house. Never had Joanie felt afraid there, despite the dark woods all around. In summer she could scarcely make out the pond, but in the short January days a huge sheet seemed spread out beyond the forest. As she rocked, it was already nearly dark out there, and the dim glow in Otis's rear attic window told her he was up in his bedroom with the door open to the stairway and storage room behind.

Her own little house had changed since her childhood in only one respect: the room her parents had slept in now was hers, four-poster and all, and her smaller room by the bath had become the quilting and stamp-collecting room, orderly at last with shelves Otis built in for her back when Landes had just departed. Joanie missed Landes, too. She and Otis had never managed to coordinate their love lives. When she was seeing someone, he wasn't, so they alternated providing a home base for each other. Landes had made a better mother than father. A meal Landes cooked was a real dinner with trimmings, not a gloppy all-purpose stew with bread to sop it up. He used their dining room, the china and silver-plated serving dishes. And then he'd play his sorts of songs on Mrs. Cable's thunky old upright — "Drink to Me Only with Thine Eyes" and "Speed, Bonny Boat" and "The Ash Grove" and "Flow Gently, Sweet Afton" and "Have You Seen But a White Lily Grow?" and, to liven things up a bit, "There Is a Tavern in the Town." On spring nights, in her worst stretches of loneliness, Joanie could sometimes hear those same tunes faintly through the trees and she'd rock and weep and stroke a cat or, if it was warm enough and not yet blackfly season, step out her front door and stand there to hear them more clearly and cry some more. She and Otis had lost their fathers first and then, within weeks of each other, their mothers; hers wasted down to nothing in the hospital in Keene, and then his fell (drunkenly, Joanie always figured) from the side of the road down into the spring runoff, which slid her into the culvert and lodged her there until she drowned.

Landes (whom Mrs. Cable had spoken of as another one of those boarders she and her son took in to help with expenses after her husband died) had comforted Otis, and they had both comforted Joanie. They had become her parents, and for a while she was a little girl again, a funny little girl who liked to pore over her stamps with her big magnifying glass or sew at her patchwork in fierce silence. What was it, Otis had always wondered, about her patterns of squares? A sheet of commemoratives and a quilt weren't all that unlike. Sit on a pan, Otis! she'd say, the palindrome she'd taunted him with ever since fifth grade. Patterns of squares? Hmm. Oh, she supposed she liked order, or at least a certain kind of order: matching things up. Wasn't her whole job a delicate matching up of things? This thin envelope from a distant shore (or more likely from Massachusetts) finds its way to a doorstep in Otis Pond, slips in the slot, the basket, the aluminum box; another connection is made, a slow webbing across time, physical, tangible — nothing like phone lines where sound is instant or video screens whose light is seized from the air. The letter must make its fragile way in the world, and it needs a Joanie, local representative of an international system, to hold it, press it, find its home.

Sharon suddenly leapt to the floor. Was Otis's tramping of the path sending a subtle vibration to her tiny ear? If only it were Chris — the thought swept over Joanie. Why wasn't it Chris tramping up her hill now? Why was she home with her loudmouth brood, tearing them away from Nintendo to their fatherless supper table? Oh! Joanie shivered and embraced her own bosom, then steeled herself. Voices of Sunny and Dick and a laugh from Otis were nearing through the woods.

Old friends, conscious of one another all their lives, so little otherwise distracted by the burgeoning world, feeling instead held close within a constant one, where a new automobile in the mill parking lot marked a minor epoch, where an untried brand of cereal at the store brought excitement, where a stone was never turned up by frost without remark, a tree never died unmourned — these friends in this village had spent so much time together over their nearly five decades that an approach to a door felt more like absorption into the wall of a cell: a merging of chromosomes, forever recombining, splitting, attaching — an organism with its own single subconscious essence, the formality and loneliness of its discrete manifestations merely aspects of a complete pattern intuited by each.

And so they were all suddenly there. They were soon warmed, then heartily fed, as the cats (old friends, too) wove their sinuous threads around them, knotting up here, snipping off there.

Later, Joanie got the potbelly stove heating up the living room, kettle boiling atop it; the Reichardts finished doing the dishes while Otis checked out the drip in Joanie's bathtub. She took her mother's tea things off the mantel. Joanie was being her mother, now. Her mother filled her body up. No one saw how every careful move she made — pouring, placing the spoon, plopping the sugar cube, stirring — was her mother's. She would be Joanie as soon as the others came in to sit and sip. But now no one in the universe knew it wasn't her mother in that small living room, opening the tin of shortbreads, tucking one golden rectangle on each saucer, shooing a cat, setting the steaming cups on the side table around the bright yellow pile of *National Geographics*. It wouldn't be long before talk was echoing around again.

Joanie sat. Cats came. Then she called, and the faucets running in bathroom and kitchen both shut off. "Fixed,"

Otis declared. "All done," said Dick, wiping his hands. And Sunny was starting to chatter, even before she sat down again, about the deal of thinking she'd been doing since Christmas, and though she knew she wasn't a thinker by nature, she was latching onto something at last, something about Sam, and she'd promised Dick she'd try to explain it to her friends tonight because Dick was going crazy with her always talking about Sam, as if she'd never really got past him, as if it was all rushing back to mess up their marriage after twenty-five years. Joanie's old mother sailed swiftly back to her graveyard hillock and crawled in under deep blankets of snow.

And Sunny heaved out a "Well!" after she'd secured everyone's attention. Her bright eyes darted from Otis on the ladder-back chair to Dick close beside her on the sagging couch to Joanie imperceptibly rocking, one cat per thigh. "Dick's going to kill me," Sunny said, "but I have to talk to my oldest friends, don't I, about the little issue we've been having? I could never talk to Ann and Peter, they're such a tight pair." "I'm glad to know we single folk are good for something," quipped Joanie, and Dick gave a sympathetic smile. He was a hardworking man; he'd loved Sunny Aldridge all his life, waited while she carried on with Sam (and others) figuring ministers' daughters were expected to be a little wild; he'd waited till the competition had dwindled to Ed Forgan and Otis Cable, and then, when it suddenly seemed more important than anything else to Sunny to have a baby, once more he'd offered his devotion. Dick's own personality, which was marked generally by unruffled cheerfulness and a steady slow pace, occasionally flared to considerable proportions. Sunny said he was the

only man who'd ever really terrified her, and that included
Sam Lara. Sam hadn't ever been scary, actually; his sexual
exuberance was a thing to enjoy not fend off. In fact, that
distinction now appeared at the heart of what Sunny had
been mulling over in her recent uncharacteristic soul-
searching: "Well, lately, I've been remembering Sam a lot
as he was back when," she said, drawing Otis and Joanie
toward her with that breathy melting voice her boyfriends
had seemed to find so tremendously seductive. "Over the
years," she said, "you've all made me think he used to be
something awful. But my year with Sam — oh, it wasn't
even a year! And then my abortion — *that* wasn't any fun,
I promise you — but that time was mostly all a hell of a
lot of fun. I can't think of it like you others do. You were
already hating Sam then. Dick, you did, you always did,
and Peter after he stopped being Sam's best friend did,
too, and Otis, you were always looking for Sam's weak
spots and even when you found them you blamed it all on
Sam. But here's what none of you could see: that Sam's
got a different feeling about his — well, I can say it — his
body. All right?" She looked at their blank faces and realized she'd have to refine her terms: "As if his body doesn't
belong to him entirely. He used to test it out, his body,
doing all sorts of things, diving, running, speeding, fight-
ing — I don't mean just sex. To see if he could kill it or see
if he could hurt it. And if he did, would that mean hurting
his actual self or just the body? All right, you think I'm
peculiar. But I imagine his body was always making him
do things he maybe didn't really want to. Sometimes it
was even good things like wrestling the Forgans' mutt off
Mrs. Paulson's Siamese or when he was back in the village

once for spring vacation how he painted his mother's front porch in one single day. He just had to do it, that's what he said. You guys were inside your own bodies always, plop, just like that. I was, too. Then I spent one whole night out in the woods with Sam and it began to feel like I almost didn't even have a body. It was so dark and I couldn't see a thing but stars, and it was more like how in church my invisible soul has these amazing feelings inside just my head — "

"You can imagine," said Dick, nodding toward Joanie, "I'm not crazy about hearing Sunny relive her teenage love-making sessions." "I'm not sure I'm crazy about it either, Dick," said Joanie. "Oh you people!" Sunny huffed, tossing her small frame against the back of the couch, the exasperated little girl, another facet of her seductive routine. But presently she became again a serious grown woman in her forties, a woman who lately had been going back to church — not to the village's only congregation, which since her father's day had been without a regular pastor and was now visited on alternate Sundays by the Reverend Bobby Forrester from across the county line, and not to that Unitarian church near Keene with the woman minister where the Ottos and Dokes and Mac Rhodes and even the Bodmans went, but to a small cement-block church out the post road, the House of the Lord, a place which her father would scorn if he were alive but which had been embraced of late by Sunny, even if not by Dick, a place full of people from back roads and trailer homes, from junctions and forks that considered even Otis Pond one of the real towns. It wasn't precisely that Sunny had got religion, but she was always getting *something* new at regular intervals throughout her life, and this time it was a tightly packed room of people she studied anthropologically as much as spiritually; Sunny could rage with them over our declining moral universe on Sundays and get some laughs out of them Mondays over lunch in the post office. She accommodated both points of view, believer and cynic; she had, in one sense, the largest mind in town, not in intellectual candlepower, perhaps, but in all-encompassing spirit. Or maybe she was just a nut. In either case, in Joanie Voshell's living room, Sunny now held her listeners rapt. What long-undetected essence of the intimate life of Sam Lara mightn't she be about to expand upon?

"I don't want to be rude, " she said solemnly. Otis and Joanie fortified themselves as she proceeded: "But all of a sudden, you can't seem to get away from, you know, ho-mo-sexuality." She pronounced it gingerly like that, uncertain of the word's effect, then quickly plunged on: "It's all over my radio — the religious shows and the psychology experts and the people calling in. Of course, I'm used to you two, but when there was all that in the paper about Jim Ezzelino and his videos, I was thinking, well, now it's come to our little neck of the woods, all that stuff I keep hearing about out there. Now, I'm ready to believe it about Ezzelino, but definitely not Sam. He's a different story. I should know. I don't believe for one minute he's ever been with that Arab boy, not in that way."

Sunny's sense of Sam's unruly body apparently didn't extend quite that far. Otis was shaking his head at his old schoolmate, the girl a grade below him who pretended to misspell words to give herself the chance for some intense agonizing, for eyelash-batting hopeful squeals and then a cute little tantrum — the person he once envied most of anyone in the village.

"All right, Otis," she said, "you probably think otherwise, just like Dick. You think Sam's finally come home with another guy, just like you always wanted him to." With a wry smile Otis said, "A little late for my purposes, though."

Joanie looked distressed, and her cats felt it; Sharon slunk off her knee, and Nelson (named for Pop, the old postmaster) stretched, rump in air, and sprang after. Joanie knew Otis found all this no joking matter, yet he was absolutely cool, sitting straight on that uncomfortable chair, his Indian cheeks smooth as ever, his mustache sparse, the scruffy mop he chopped and snipped at randomly, when he felt it needed it, throwing a black shadow across his brow and black eyes. Surely, he hadn't meant to sound so predatory; he was only playing up to Sunny's likely notion of ho-mo-sexuals. He liked to disarm her candor by going her one better. They'd been slipping around each other that way for years.

And yet Joanie knew Otis truly was, in some regard, nearly as mysterious as Sam. She'd hardly known half of what had passed between those two boys when they were teenagers. For all Otis's confidences, some inner thing remained unstated. A self-deprecatory lowering of chin, a dismissive shake of head, a twisted lip — these formed his stern line of defense. Joanie respected it. But whereas Sam's opacity could veil the slightest quiver of a nerve, Otis would, on a few occasions, turn translucent, and Joanie could see all the way in to his beating heart; it was there, and she'd known of it long before any of the rest, who

judged him ever aloof and independent — the village brain.
Joanie alone knew he was also something warmer: the village memory, the one who linked together the past through
his schoolboy obsession for codifying the inheritances, the
land transfers, the intermarrying families, all those complex patterns of descent and property etched in the granite
tombstones by the pond. Old Mrs. Otto in her history had
left merely a linear record — the Thorne family, then the
Dokes, the Nelsons, the Rhodeses — but Otis, young Otis
Cable, the boy who hadn't finished his last year of school
but had gone to work in his disabled father's stead, that
boy knew the true weave, the hidden loops, the unravel-
ings — not *through* time, year by year, but *over* time, suspended in a web that might capture the spirit of Elder
August Thorne held fast beside some child of the future
dawdling in the graveyard. These weavings, which he had
sought to know and remember and live within, Otis could
never abandon for a foreign land. If he had finished school,
gone on to college — even if only over to Keene State —
how might he ever have placed himself upon the fabric of
the outside world? Yet — and this was a sadness Joanie
knew from her own yearnings — how few opportunities
might Otis ever have to find himself a companion within
the small circle of the village? Joanie had some knowledge
of the lonely forays of his adult years to find a loving soul,
a breathing body to bring home to his native valley; she
even had some familiarity with the fervent letters back
and forth, the wishes, the pleas, the rare episodes of harmony. Eventually, Landes had stayed longest, had become
part of village life, if not finally woven in for good. And
over that period, Otis's intermittent translucency had

shone more steadily on Joanie. Others sensed it, too. Nothing was said, but a kind of relief spread through the villagers, to see Otis a happier man. Questions weren't asked who this Landes was, in his coat and tie driving his Chevy Nova off to Keene every morning, but his polite solicitude of other shoppers at the store, his speaking up intelligently in town meeting, his cheerful greeting of Fred Otto when their ways crossed on the plaza all revealed a benign new spirit among us. He wouldn't turn out like that phone lineman whose van used to trundle up the pond road after dusk and rattle out again at six before Mac Rhodes even opened up, or like that seldom-seen ex-con (as Joanie alone had known him to be) who slept a lot and drank a lot with Mrs. Cable and didn't make it through one winter. No, Landes was a new thread to adorn the pattern. It isn't with children alone, as Joanie well knew, that the design keeps complicating itself; that's a false notion born, no doubt, of the pride and effort of parental experience. But to village memory, existing in uniform perpetual space, inheritances are never merely a business of genetics. The soul of a village is a more intricate concoction and the ways in which personalities form themselves uncountable. Our village breathed with Landes as much as ever it did with the little Dokes and Grandys and Paulsons; they breathed with Landes and he with them. We are their chidren, they are ours — all of us. It is only in cities, Joanie imagined, that parenthood becomes such a lonely endeavor. Ah, poor Chris!

Joanie woke from these thoughts. Sunny was still peppering Otis with her convictions about Sam's instinctive sexuality. Her practiced eye was reviewing all the nuances of his most vulnerable susceptibilities. Dick, looking par-

ticularly thick and stodgy now, was keeping his own counsel. Joanie caught his glance. "All right," he said and
clapped his hands suddenly. "That's enough. Say, why don't
you two just go together and take Sam for yourselves, one
from the front and one from behind?" "Dick!" Sunny was
professing monstrous shock, her eyes wide, her fingertips
held delicately to her lips. "You see, Joanie," her husband
went on, "after four kids and two decades at the mill, Sunny
wonders if life mightn't have gone another way. Well, so
don't I! So doesn't everyone, I suppose. It's her new churchy
friends. I bet she's fixing to be the one to save Sam Lara
from the abominations of Sodom. She's going to snare that
man back into the ways of the Lord before the Arab boy
gets him for good." "Oh Dick," sputtered Sunny, "Sam
never sodomized anything. What do *you* know!" "Sunny,
my love, Sam's been to Sodom and back, I promise you.
Hasn't he, Otis?"

Joanie, who'd been about to put in her two cents, hadn't
expected Dick to turn the question to their silent friend.
Dick was pressing him: "I'll believe you, Otis. You can
always spot one of your fellow travelers, can't you?" Otis
had laced his fingers in front of his chin, pondering. Nelson
and Sharon, sensing the shift of attention, brushed casually
up against him with quick nudges to his ankles. But Joanie
could almost see Otis's heart emptying out.

"It was hard to figure," Otis said. "It was hard to watch.
I tried not to. For years all I might've wanted from Sam
was his assurance he would've stuck by me if he'd been
inclined that way. But now to find out his inclination at
last, that he's here in our village living with a man. I saw
their bed, Sunny. I saw them there in the candlelight."

Eyes fired with amazement, Sunny gasped, "You saw

them?" but Joanie was wondering if Otis wasn't making up all this simply to dispirit his erstwhile rival. He often made up things; even when she heard tell of his lost loves, Joanie wasn't sure what he'd lived through and what he'd merely dreamed. Sunny was soberly shaking her head. Dick tweaked her again: "Looks like Sam's body just doesn't know when to quit, Sun!"

Otis missed Nelson but scooped Sharon onto his knee. "I was walking late one night in the light snow," he said. "I was way down the post road, as far as the Quidnapunxet, so I turned back up the river road. It was cold but that dry still cold when the snow's like dust sifting down, and I'd had enough to drink to keep me warm. Those two were safe inside the Lara mill. I snuck up to the window where the shade was ripped." Joanie looked disapproving. Otis faced her. "It wasn't for the first time. I'd kept going back. I never saw enough to be entirely sure. But each shadow, each bare limb, they all swirled into one picture." "Shit!" said Sunny, but now her tantrum wasn't for show — she'd been wounded.

Dick started to chuckle, and she elbowed him, but he chuckled more and turned it to a cackle, then a hacking guffaw, and as she started pounding her fists on him, he swept it up into a howling laugh. Sunny was screeching at Dick, Sharon was struggling to escape Otis's grip and follow Nelson to safety under Joanie's bed — a great cat yawp and Otis let her go, flying through the bedroom doorway. Joanie had to shout at the Reichardts to stop their spat. When Dick was catching his breath and Sunny wringing her fingers out from the little fists they'd made, he said to her, "So maybe you'll follow me home now and hop into bed at last?" He stood up, rubbed his pummeled shoulder and smiled. "I always figured," he said, "and no offense, Otis, but I figured Sam was queer back then even. Something was sure queer about him, so why not that, too? You should've kept after him. A little more determination! As for you, Sunny, start praying, or what is it they do in that House of the Lord, stone him? Thank you, Joan, for the usual hearty feed . . ." He began layering himself in sweater, scarf, insulated vest, then hunting jacket and on top a hat with huge earflaps. From there on, it was merely a matter of getting them out the door.

That gentle osmosis of greeting, of welcoming, now reversed itself in a hasty flushing out. But all would be the same again tomorrow: the volatile Reichardts would be reabsorbed with the last representative of the Voshell line, the last Cable; Sunny would find new colors to decorate her indiscreet youth, her one season with the lost doomed romantic rebel boy, his fierce lovemaking fueled by deeper fears than she'd known. She, Sunny, had brought him closest to his transcendent self, but his unsettled innards had raveled him round and, on some Greek island, no doubt, choked the last light of Sunny out of him. That transcendence had been lost to her, too. Never reachieved with her life mate, explosive though he had — on occasion — proved himself to be, that transcendence in the dark woods, in silence under a veiled moon, was a sensation to be caught again now only in elusive memory or, perhaps briefly, in a swinging, swaying, shouting, stomping moment of prayer, all hearts beating as one, in the concrete-block church out the post road when she felt she was getting close to some great ineffable thing.

Joanie and Otis tidied up. He swiped a second shortbread out of the tin. She allowed him that. And then she walked him home, each well bundled against the cutting wind of January. Deep winter had settled in.

Their boots took them down the hard-packed snow to the pond road, icily rutted, and then across the culvert along the path to the Cable house between waving tentacles of Landes's abandoned roses. The handyman thanked the postmistress for her company; she said she'd desperately needed the air. She asked him, offhandedly, if he had told that tale of the candlelit bed for Sunny's delectation. Glove on his kitchen door latch, he turned and said, "You remember that night, too, Joanie. You drove Chris back late to Keene. You'd been with her. I confess I had a dreary little assignation of my own. And then I wandered. Walked and walked. You'd been with her, and they were with each other. Your Jeep was gone when I finally made it home. A night full of bad dreams. I had begun imagining more and more of what I didn't know or want to know or see or remember."

"After the Ottos' party? But you only had your scarf, Otis!" she said. He told her he really hadn't felt cold with all his blood pumping through him. The scene in the music room had sent him to Fred's oak cabinet for some cognac and he'd seemed to breathe fire from then on. No, he wouldn't detail his amorous enounter nor how he'd contrived to have it; one of those Italian waiters in tunic and tights, Joanie supposed, must have taken his fancy — men went about it differently from women, she knew that much. But if Otis had later seen Sam safely abed, didn't that make Sam not quite so suspect in the Ezzelino busi-

ness? Joanie somehow felt less than comfortable now saying good night to her old friend. She took it slower walking
home and found herself wondering gothically if Otis himself, to qualify as Sam's loyal redemptor, hadn't in some
fashion seen to Ezzelino's obliteration. But Otis was no
one to topple even a villain into the freezing Quidnapunxet.
Otis was a watcher like her, and a brooder. So why would
she imagine such a thing?

Ah! She realized she was atop the culvert. The whistling
wind in the pines echoed strangely hollow beneath her feet,
like the earth suffering. Down in there, she remembered,
Otis had found his mother caught between a tree limb and
the old tire they used to swing on out over the pond. She
was in a foot of water, neck unable to support her lolling
head. I mustn't indulge myself in grim visions, Joanie told
herself. These are real people. These are friends. It is our
village. Sam, too, belongs here. It's only the night and the
cold, and Sunny and Dick have thrown me out of balance
with their little exhibition. Am I so susceptible that I don't
credit what I know of the real people I've always loved,
that I can conjure up horrors just to give a goose to my
quiet life?

III

Fred Otto was feeling a lot better, but his pride had been hurt. It took him a while to realize it. Christmas Eve had all seemed still just a little dizzy. He'd tried sitting up, but after dinner, which he ate alone from the tray Judy brought him, he lay flat again, and the family gathered in the parlor to light the real candles on the tree for one nervous quarter hour, Otis monitoring them while the Ottos followed the German custom of opening presents the night before the holiday. Franklin and Sandy piped up with carols, which Sue didn't join in on because she was tackling her second slab of gingerbread with hard sauce. Brother-in-law Tim lurked in and out of the room while Gwen sat loyally by the fire leaning against her father's couch, holding on to his heavy hand. Carol insisted on keeping strictly to family rank, oldest to youngest, for the unwrappings, which became meaningless when they got down to "for the whole family" gifts from distant relations and tokens from Chamber of Commerce members (including an orange tin of amaretti di Saronno from the vanished restaurateur), but the initial few rounds had been full of thrilling surprises and yearnings satisfied — several multi-CD volumes of Byzantine music for the Franklin Ottos, a set of enormous iron saucepans and casseroles for Gwen and Tim's new condo up in Burlington, Vermont (they'd finally given up on their hippie cabin), a Nordic-Track for Sue, the actual air tickets to Florida from Fred to Carol (she wept with relief) and for Fred — well, he found himself unable to focus quite on it, but it was a huge book of designs and architectural drawings and color photographs of the buildings and inventions of Thomas Jefferson. The Ottos presented Otis with a "little something" — embarrassing for him to unwrap in front of them — a powerful set of binoculars, something which Otis had never imagined owning or even wanting but which suddenly seemed like a thing he'd always secretly craved. "To keep even better track of things than you already do," joked Carol. "Don't let me look through them," said Fred faintly from the couch, "or my eyes might fall out of my head."

And they'd given Judy a handsome woolen afghan she was still raving about when Otis passed through the kitchen, having doused the candles and brought down all the crumpled bright wrapping stuffed in a plastic bag. But Fred had confessed to Carol who'd confessed to Sue who'd confessed to Judy who now confessed to Otis that his sense of pride had been wounded by Sam Lara's behavior. Here Fred had tried his damnedest, in a situation hardly of his own making, to shelter Sam from unfair accusation, to allow him a safely private hearing, no doubt to find in his favor — because, after all, of the two it was Sam he felt closer to than the out-of-towner, it was Sam whose family had twined with his own for three generations, even if never grafting together. But Sam, so welcomed by Fred and Carol, so desired in the village, seemed angrier at his host than at his accuser. Indeed, Ezzelino scarcely seemed to matter to Sam at all.

In his dizziness, Fred had caught hold of one tiny stable particle, a lone forgotten grain of hatred for Sam Lara. He'd felt the hate even as a young man when Sam, a wicked wild adolescent, had with no provocation barred Fred's way on the gravel road by the graveyard, a little highwayman holding a fallen tree limb, jeering, challenging, spoiling for combat. Fred had tried to josh him out of it, but stubborn spindly little Sam, well beyond the term of an amusing game, had held his ground until Fred could only scoff at him and retreat to the plaza. He'd meant to visit his grandmother's recent grave. Not one to imagine an insult, Fred hadn't felt the incident as fully as he might have, but his half annoyance, his almost anger had compacted itself into a small seed, dormant through the seasons but forever vital.

Fred's determination to demand an accounting of Jim Ezzelino from Sam's lips came early in the new year. If Sam had had no part in the man's failure to show up, he could surely say so. He *must* say so — and prove it. Otherwise, as rumor made only too logical a case, it was likely that whatever Sam had wanted to stifle might indeed be so monstrous as to have driven him to further crime here at the very scene of his youthful delinquency. How mild the smashing of a mill window, the burning of a diving float, even the abandonment of a seduced and pregnant girl might now seem compared with the unknown act that Fred was determined to uncover.

Who else but Sam had cause to fear Jim Ezzelino? Mysteries are meat for curious villagers, who can never know too much about one another or suspect too little. Sam's seeming friendlessness was all the more evident in his middle age, when to sift through childhood's battles with old enemies marks a deep historic bond, a new sort of friendship as cherished as any other; Sam was disinclined to indulge in such reminiscence, and so, it seemed, his enmity must still hold. He shied back from confidence, he had as yet made no effort to wake the love of his former compatriots. One began to wonder (or at least Fred did) how the sweeping fierceness in Sam's soul had been sustained at such heat all these years? Where had his once reluctant tongue learned to lacerate so keenly? He had gained practice in human warfare in his far travels, apparently. Sam knew the strategic arts: where a single word might once have kindled in him a blind capricious rage and another word, as easily, stilled it, now his soul seemed unmixed, at work deep within itself, concentrating all its force on mercilessness.

Thus, in his recuperation, Fred mulled over the effect Sam still seemed to have on him. Carol was making him take it easy, stay home from the mill, leave it to Peter Doke to manage and take the load off his own neck for a time. But while taking pleasure in the Jefferson book and in an elaborate tome about wooden shipbuilding sent by his sister in Boston, Fred's thoughts kept fluttering back to the perceived insult from Sam. It's easier to condemn than praise, Fred admitted. For all the months of nudging himself toward liking the returned wanderer, one day only had sufficed to raise a storm in his heart against him.

And something worried Fred Otto even more, the faded

memory of a peculiar note of jealousy that had always sounded in the air around his youthful encounters with Sam Lara. When Sam had finished prep school and Fred was nearing thirty, he'd felt it, and indeed he'd felt it throughout his twenties, ever since he first became aware of that explosive little Sammy Lara having turned — somewhere around age ten — into a mean young bastard who now (this was the aggravating part) commanded even more attention and also an unaccountable measure of respect in the town. Had Fred Otto ever done a single reprehensible thing? He who stood as heir to his father's mill, who would someday employ half the people who moped and shuffled about him, though he was always their faithful support, was generally shunned in jocular discourse. But Sam Lara, for all anyone had known at the time (when old Gerald Lara was presumed near retirement), would even sooner employ another substantial portion of villagers, and no one stepped deferentially around *him*. If they treated Sam cautiously it was with a kind of awe, or fear, not resentment or disdain. Yes, even the eleven-year-old Sam, voice beginning to crack (earlier than Fred's ever had), little tufts emerging under his white arms as he swung the monkey rings in the schoolyard, that Sam had a magnetism his rotten behavior did nothing to weaken. Indeed, kindly Fred could scarcely command attention at all, while Sam's name was on everybody's lips. And dammit if it still wasn't! Sam needed only return to Otis Pond and resume his position as rebel prince, made all the more romantic now because his castle was in ruins, and he was one of the people again, while his vine-covered dilapidated empty-echoing hall still conferred on him the stature of a chieftain. His serfs, having long gone unemployed, forgetting what servitude they once owed the Lara clan, now with their unhoped for (but unforgotten) lord returned to his ancestral seat, would surely march again under his bright banner. They hadn't thirty years to think back on of Sam denying them paid sick leave or stinting on merit raises or pension plans.

The more Fred let his mind soar into fantastic realms, the dizzier he felt — and he had another acute episode on January second, but then his new determination took hold: Sam must answer for the absence of Jim Ezzelino. The police had done little beyond their obligatory questioning; it was a raw crop of troopers — what did they know of the Terror of the Post Road, circa 1960?

Fred only later learned of how Mrs. Paulson, wheeling her grandchild down along the river on a miraculous day of January thaw, had appeared at Sam Lara's door, confessing a modest need. She'd always remembered his rescue of the great-great-great-great-great-grandfather of her current old tom from the jaws of Mutt Forgan. In winter it was hard keeping warm — this sunny melting day excepted — and she daren't go to Mr. Otto, who'd been ill himself. In short, her oil was out and she'd used up what wood she had for her Franklin stove and her daughter who'd married a Griffin (perhaps Sam remembered him) hadn't much to spare. Oh, he'd been so kind, she told Joanie Voshell when she'd trudged back up to the village, he'd said he'd order up a full tank for her, think nothing of it. "You know, Joanie," Mrs. Paulson went on, tucking her sleeping grandchild's curls back under his knit cap, "he's so lonesome down there. It's dreary in those dripping woods. The river was misting and the mill looked like an old shell of itself.

It was all dark and wet and chill. I hear he never sleeps at night. Remember that nightmare fit he had when he first was back here? When Ed found him? Oh, I suspect he still doesn't sleep well. Imagine the horrible things he's seen out there in the world. You know, I don't really care whatever it was he did that was supposed to be so dreadful. What business was it of that Ezzelino fellow? Sam's back home safe now where he should be. He takes care of us, so we'll take care of him, too, won't we? I have a soft spot for Sam. I know he was an impossible child — " Here she lost herself a few seconds, gazing at her own innocent charge, whom her daughter didn't want to consign yet to Sunny's day care, what with her bored and eager retired mom to rely on, a luxury few had. Mrs. Paulson was quite opposed to Fred Otto's attempts at social reorganization anyway — retirement apartments, company doctors, the mill athletics program; it all made inroads on family responsibility, she thought. An application to the fallen lord suited her temperament better, and indeed it suited Sam; to dispense a favor, not part of any ordained system, became his spontaneous pleasure.

And these pleasures grew from one another. Mrs. Paulson was only the first beneficiary of charitable Sam. Word spread. The posthumous coffers of Gerald Lara, wisely maintained by a trust officer in Keene, seemed capable of rescuing many a villager from destitution's brink, but only when required to afford a specific commodity. Sam would hire Otis Cable to repair the frozen pipes of Grandmother Grandy, Sam would come to the village hall to call a tow truck to extricate Kathee Thompson's older brother's Citation from a snow bank, would take Ed Forgan's simple-

minded cousin to the post road mall for dental care. These
generous acts, if such they were, were done under Fred
Otto's very nose. Eventually he couldn't escape word of
them. When he sounded off to Carol, she tried to put it in
perspective: "But what else has he got to do with his
money, Fred? It probably makes him feel respectable at last.
Besides, it's relatively small potatoes. It's you they owe
their livelihoods to. Don't be jealous, honey." But Fred was
afraid his rival was slowly, sneakily buying them off.

And what of the manifold rumors — mysterious doings
in the sands of Arabia, silent rubouts in our own peaceful
New Hampshire? Unconfirmed, they almost added luster
to Lara's name. Otis Ponders had so little sense of foreign
lands, it seemed natural, perhaps, to picture Sam warding
off a Pathan horde with shining steel. And if, in accom-
plishing his lawless deeds, he'd done something mortally
to offend some tourist named James Ezzelino — oh, even
selling an Italian boy, let's say, to a desert sheik (who can
begin to imagine the perversity enountered in the Persian
Gulf?) and in exhange (invent a good story, now!) bringing
back a brown-skinned young Arab of his very own, for
Sam's lustiness had run through just about every other
variation — and if this had so enraged Ezzelino (who'd
wanted the boy, either the Italian or the Arab, for himself,
no doubt), then who's to blame Sam for concluding the
battle, at last, on his native soil? To think that one of us,
a man we know, had escaped the law in a distant country
and come home only to escape it here as well! Something
splendid about it. Casa Ezzelino and its catering service
didn't belong in Otis Pond; the Ottos had meant it all as
a treat, we know — they're like that — but what do we

want with squid and anchovies in this mountain valley? Sam is ours. His money comes from us, from this rushing river of ours and its two basins of stillness, the Ottos' big pond with its deep surges and, farther down, the woodland pool of Lara, its gentler but still fervent pressure pouring through the rusty old locks enough to fire up a few dim bulbs, anyway. And if Sam is a criminal, our money isn't. He holds it safe for us in his outlaw hands, because without him it might now leave us forever, and we'd be stuck with the modernizing Ottos, ready to bring in any new high-rent operation that made business sense. Already they'd torn down the Lara homestead, with its bowed balconies and sagging porches, for a row of blank boxes to store us in till we died. We need a man capable of murder — or of self-defense, anyway. We'll protect him.

Were these the true thoughts of the village or merely Fred Otto's paranoid imaginings on a sleepless night? One morning when Otis was shoveling off the steps, Fred tried to sound him on the current temper of things, but Otis, as always, after hearing him out, held his own idea close and let slip but a few words, as he leaned against a pillar of the eastern porte cochere: "You never know about these things, Mr. Otto. People are finicky." Cold vapor from his lips. "You think they're doing just fine, you think all's well, and then it turns out they're not. That's why I do so much reading. It's the closest I get to understanding people." "But people in books aren't . . ." "Because," Otis explained, "you've got the author there to make some sense of them." "But we haven't got an author here," joked Fred, "or at least we Unitarians don't know what to make of one." Otis drew in his breath and collected a thought: "It's the Otto family," he said, "that brought all the books to town. If there's one thing in my life I'll always be grateful for, it's that."

"Thank you, Otis," said Fred, genuinely warmed by the thought. He looked around his study, when he got back inside, and concluded he had read a lot himself, not as much as Otis, at least not of the strictly literary sort of thing, but he did remember his poets from school and college. They'd stuck with him. How better to fall asleep at night than to sample a lyric of Keats or Wordsworth and drift off in the embrace of its music?

But what had troubled Fred Otto most of all, that week late in January, had been word of Sam Lara throwing a dinner party. He'd heard it from, of all people, Joanie Voshell when she dropped off his mail. She'd been invited, the younger Troyer boy with his girlfriend Emily Grandy as well — and there were others: Ed Forgan, some Paulsons. Fred had actually wandered out, he confessed to Otis (who brought him his lunch tray by the study fire) — yes, when it had got good and dark and no none was on the road, he'd taken his first long walk since his illness all the way down the river to the Lara mill. What could he see but light gleaming out one window of the hall where the sailcloth shade had been pulled back? Fred hadn't dared step closer. But he wanted to enter, to demand, to accuse. Electricity supplied a steady brightness, but there flared also a great fire in the open stove at the far end of the room and smoke poured from the chimney, its sweet scent drifting even to Fred's cold nostrils. "I stood there making myself madder and madder," he told Otis. "But I'm not so rude as to interrupt a dinner party. You know, it made me think of a snatch of poetry I'd chanced on a few nights before," Fred said, thinking partly to impress Otis and (he trusted) amuse him. "It went something like

> Far checkering o'er the picture window, plays
> The unwanted faggot's hospitable blaze;
> And gay retainers gather round the hearth,
> And something something and with eyes of mirth."

Otis shook his head forgivingly. "The unwanted faggot, eh?" "An apt double entendre," said Fred, "it certainly leapt out at me! I found myself pronouncing the word 'faggot' with some venom. I don't mean to offend, Otis. It's not my general feeling." "No, sir," said Otis, "and I guess everyone's got a gay retainer or two around the place." The men chuckled. Harmony, humor, after all. "By the way, did *you* know Sam had thrown a party, Otis? Joanie Voshell must have told you." "Well, the fact is," said Otis, "I was a guest there myself."

IV

And they were to see each other soon again, naturally enough, in the library. Sam never lingered there. He had volumes to return and was quickly ready with the next ones to borrow. He'd gone through Tennyson and now was on to *The Ring and the Book*. "Italian intrigue seems to appeal to you," said Otis, instantly realizing his provocative intent. Sam threw him a dark-browed glance.

At that dinner nothing had been mentioned of Ezzelino's challenge or his disappearance, no private word had passed between Otis and his unaccustomed host to remind them of the morning before Christmas in Fred Otto's study, when an occasional but loyal employee had never abandoned his part-time boss's side. As at age ten, Otis knew still when to leave Sam to his thoughts and when to answer a request to fix a broken water pipe or accept an offhand invitation to dinner at the old mill. And now it occurred to him in the library that he might even invite Sam — unprecedented act — back to his own quiet house for a late afternoon pot of tea, perhaps with a drop of brandy in it, with no Khaled hovering behind his chair, ciphering the babble of English.

"And you?" queried Sam. But what was he asking? Oh. Otis remembered he was holding a book in his own hands as well. "I'm sailing about the Pacific," he said. "I started in on *Typee* and *Omoo* and now I'm on to *Mardi*." "Sailing?" "They're Melville's sea tales. Perhaps," Otis said cautiously, "I've been delving into stories of wayfarers to imagine what it was like for you, out in the wide world."

Sam's expression lightened. He swept his grizzled hair from his eyes. He hadn't cut his hair since coming home and was approaching his old shagginess. Sam seemed, possibly, touched by Otis's current motive for reading. Now was the moment: the quondam suitor risked an invitation, and it was, very casually, accepted.

Stepping into the bitter cold (Sam encased in his sheepskin, Otis in many layers of sweaters and a baggy denim jacket), the two turned together onto the gravel road up along the graveyard; the narrower pondside path lay under deep snow, as did the wide windswept pond itself, only a few paw prints from village dogs and perhaps a fisher marten marring the perfect whiteness. The road crested almost as high as the gravestones themselves, each with its lintel of white snow, and then — after a momentary shiver passed through each man (probably just the cold, but conceivably in remembrance of times years ago when one had found the other up there alone, cogitating with his soul) — they descended past the cluster of houses and cast glances up at the beetling hill of the Ottos, the loggia looming just above a granite outcropping. The sun in the west played on the marble and brick and slate and glass to remind Sam and Otis, boys again for an instant, of their origins, humbler and yet much humbler still, as they walked on toward the pond road.

Otis worried that Joanie would somehow glance out her window up there in the woods and see him with Sam again. Crossing the culvert, its grim significance unknown to Sam, they approached the tall thin house. A thorn waving high on one mad shoot snagged Sam's hair, but he soon disentangled himself. "Aren't your ears cold?" Otis asked solicitously. "Sometimes I think my ears are stone," said Sam. Curious thought. Was he saying "Oh, don't worry about me" or confessing a shameful debility? Sam, Sam, Sam went rushing through Otis's brain, all the old attachment, all the deep old sadness.

They entered at the kitchen door and sat at the table looking out at the pond. "It hasn't changed," said Sam. "Even the same toaster you had to open the sides of." Sam had entered Otis's house a handful of times in their youth, unbidden, unannounced, each instance a clear memory for Otis, but that he should recognize the toaster seemed miraculous. "What's this?" he said next, picking up the binoculars case and withdrawing from it the instrument itself. "You spy on moonlight skinny-dippers with these?" "Oh, not in this weather," said Otis. Humor again — as with Fred, if only to keep it all buoyant, keep it possible. Sam had peeled off his heavy sheepskin and stowed it on the third chair. The fourth, beside Otis, was piled with newspapers tied in bundles. The kettle whistled, the water was poured upon the tea ball, the spot of brandy administered and the steeping pot brought to the metal-top table with the tin mugs.

"How do you ever fill up this place?" Sam asked, each

of them watching the dark green ceramic pot, as if imagining how inside it secretly brewed its potion. "I live just in here mostly, winters anyway," Otis explained. "The second floor, my mother's room and my father's, I've closed them off, except for the john. The attic's cozier." "And when your friend was here?" "Well, after my mother died, he tried moving down. His room went back to being a storeroom, and he took my mother's. Felt sort of strange. And he used my father's for his studio. North light." "A painter?" "He thought he was," said Otis, "you know, as a hobby. It all looked like oatmeal mush to me." "Oh, that sort of painter," said Sam. "Any samples?" "I made him take every god-damned ugly one of them with him," Otis declared.

Then he poured, and Sam raised his mug. "A better future," he said and touched the rim to Otis's mug, but before Otis could bring his tea to his lips, Sam had sipped and was puffing air to cool his mouth and the steaming surface. So Otis watched the steam rise from his mug and found himself listening, for the first time since Sam had returned, to a tale unfolding of the unknown East where Sam had strayed. "I've spent a lot of time over cups of tea these many years," Sam began. "Coffee, too, of course. But in the Arabian Sea, on an island, the other side of the world from here, oh, lots of tea." "Was Khaled there with you?" Otis dared to ask. "First time, no. But I took him back there. An island's like a village, Otis. Nowhere much to go. I felt at home. We lived very peacefully there. But the first time I was there all alone. A hut on a beach. It's still possible in parts of the world. It's not so exotic, it wasn't even especially beautiful. It was just peaceful. A cup of tea

lasted a long while. And the sun would be going down.
Very dry, very still. But I'd gotten into some unpleasant
circumstances, and this was an escape." "You won't tell
me about Khaled?" Otis asked with overt hesitance, wanting Sam to see how tender the question was for them both.
Very slowly, pausing between words, Sam said, "I'd thought
you'd be pleased to find Khaled with me." Otis squinted
across the tabletop. "You're giving me a glimpse," he said,
"of how your life has been. And I have a glimpse of how
it is now. And you once gave me a glimpse years ago of
you, of your own self, Sam. But these glimpses . . ." Otis
couldn't complete the phrase. He sipped at his tea now.

"When I first saw you again," Sam said, softly and simply,
without that note of inwardness he employed to cloak his
usual speech, "I asked you to forgive me." "No," said Otis,
"you said you had never forgiven *yourself*." "Oh, that's
how I said it? But I meant them both." "And what's Khaled,
then," Otis wanted to know, "your act of contrition?" "Oh,
I see," Sam said, regretfully almost. "But I thought you
might be pleased with Khaled. I'm back here now at home,
Otis, one of the faithful." "You'll go no more a-roving,"
Otis nearly sang, because it was a line from one of Landes's
songs that had been haunting the back of his brain lately.
"Do you love me or do you hate me, Otis?" Sam asked him
point-blank, setting his mug, clank, on the metal table.
Otis raised his black eyes to pierce Sam through. He knew
he'd pondered the same question himself many years ago
and got an answer for it, a knife blade to his bare throat.
But even that answer was no answer. It could have meant
either. And after what they had nearly consummated, how
could it have meant anything certain but a sort of instinc-

tual terror? And now Sam was pondering, desperately, the same question, and Otis couldn't answer him either, not with knife blade but neither with an embrace. Otis had, only, another question: "How could you bring a man here with you?" and Sam, then, had yet only another question for him: "How could I bring a woman?"

The vision rose of Sam on his Arabian island. So it wasn't in Greece that the transformation had occurred. Island, no, isle — no, not even as sea-cradled as that word sounded — islet, that was the word, something terribly small and featureless and parched. A bare bone of an islet of sand. Stripped to the bone. Where the idea of woman, at last, evaporated into the bluest of skies, and the idea of man rose before him. No longer a creature unlike him and unfathomable but one with his own skin and own heart and own thought. His fellow man. Khaled. What, a pearl diver? Dripping from the sea. The tale kept unwinding itself in Otis's humming brain. He couldn't turn back a page of it. Adventures poured forth: the rescue in a storm, the flight on horseback over hot sands, the flashing blades, the hurled stones, the labyrinthine alleyways and tunnels of escape, the lush couches, thick carpets, silken pillows, the incense smoking, the steaming cups of Arabian tea, the rings on fingers, bells on toes, music wherever he goes, dancing girls — or were they boys, really? — and the pasha himself, puffing on a long pipe, thick eyelids lowered, a haze of smoke and steam and sandstorm and weary limbs and lust fulfilled and too many figs and dates and cakes and olives and sleep and sleep . . .

"You know," came Sam's own voice from beyond the fading vision, "Otis, you know I had nothing to do with this Ezzelino disappearing." Otis sat back in the creaky chair and looked pondward. Dusk. The snow was pinkish here, there bluish. "Fred Otto came to me today," Sam went on. "He was as polite as can be. He stood at my door and waited for Khaled to fetch me. I came there covered with sawdust from my work and looked at him. He told me he thought I owed it to him and to the village and to the Casa Ezzelino people and the police and whoever else to account for the man who was missing. But how can I account for a man I saw for only a quarter of an hour who seems to think I implicated him in a smuggling operation or cheated him in the flesh trade or who ran afoul of some damn indiscretion of mine I couldn't possibly recall from my long sinful life? I told Fred I could account for myself, that was all. He wanted to know if I had witnesses as to my whereabouts later on in the night before Christmas Eve." "Witnesses?" said Otis, coming back from his dream, but now almost directly entering another, a dream of entwined naked arms and legs, which he had forcibly to shut out. Sam's voice: "I told fucking Fred Otto I'd gone home with Khaled who was my witness and would swear by Allah or Vishnu or any other god he asked him to invoke." The familiar curling lip approached the smile it quickly evaded. "But that's not good enough for old fucking Fred. Here's what he said: 'I suspect that boy would swear to anything.'" Sam snorted his fierce exasperation. "And so, Otis," he added after a long deep breath and a toss of his gray locks — and here it became apparent why he had come so readily to the Cable house, why he had told of his seagirt sanctuary in the East, why he had tried to find in Otis some fellowship as companions of the faithful — "I need you to swear for me, too. By the great spirit Manitou, by the happy hunting ground Ponemah, you name it. Swear to fucking Fred that you know me, Otis, you know where I was. Otis? What's it all matter anyway? I've done nothing. Just shut Fred up, please. Otis, do you love me? Do you hate me?"

Both, and for all time, Otis would have said if he could have. But the mug was dry, the sun was set, Sam had Khaled to return to, Otis would sit there alone, eat the last of his Christmas pears, read, listen to night sounds — the wind across the pond and whirring in the pines. "If I had not, myself, been somewhere else with, I'm afraid, witnesses of my own who might contradict me," he said as mysteriously as he could, "I would swear anything for you, Sam. But I can't." And then, with his own kind of slight smile: "Of course I love you, Sam."

V

There had developed in Otis Pond, New Hampshire, a murmur of civic unrest — oh, nothing at all like what was seething in the metropolises to the south and west. Race was no factor here nor was creed, the public school system wasn't, thievery wasn't, drugs and disease and gang violence weren't; even money (worrisome as it could be) was not so scarce as to engender revolt; besides, in a pinch, we villagers could always turn to the charitable Mr. Lara if there wasn't enough spilling over from our usual benefactor. But a new confusion arose even in that regard. Frederick Otto, for all too long, had been the sole seigneur, his generosity unquestioned, unequaled, unchallenged. With the reappearance of Samuel Lara, the very idea of an alternative revived in our imaginations. None of those Tarnoff-Rices, Bodmans, and Januses, despite ex-urban bankrolls, had ever seemed contesters for power; the Ottos had absorbed them under welcoming wings: good for the village, infusions of purchasing power, extra sources of odd jobs. But now, with Sam back, the newcomers were cast in a less favorable light: toadies at the court of Otto, invited to the hilltop house for "drinks" or "just a little family supper" while we could only serve there. But Sam, in his search for communion (if that was what he sought), invited *us*. Yes, even Ed Forgan came to dine and drink, and if he had to be tossed out when midnight struck, it was all in good humor, guest and host both drunk as lords. Of course, Khaled wasn't drunk. Khaled didn't, wouldn't drink — not more than a sip of wine as a toast — but he listened wide-eyed to tales of his master's youth, how Ed used to egg him on to ever faster velocities riding sidecar in one of Sam's more precarious vehicles, and all the pranks played by best pals Sam and Peter (the Dokes were at that particular dinner, too) in the shining hour of their camaraderie.

"I don't know how Peter escaped jail in those days," Ann mused. "Why did only Sam land in the clink and Pete just slink off home?" "Because," her husband explained, "I knew just the point to stop. It was always on that one last foray — one more six-pack, one more rock to throw — that Sam got nabbed." "But, Sam," said Ann, "why the hell didn't you ever rat on him?" The possibility had, clearly, never occurred to Sam. Why should he get anyone else in trouble? It was trouble he sought, for himself. If he had it alone, it was all the more poignant. Let him feel the chase, the capture, the accusation, the punishment, the eventual release — and then the enticement all over again. Let him savor each phase. A tagalong was welcome but expected to flee as part of the staging. He himself was the criminal, singular and glorious — not in the world's eye (who cared?) but in his own, his veritable orgasm of private, secret, inmost masturbatory gloriousness. And who could you rat on for that?

"It puzzles me," said Peter, now middle-aged and portly, leaning back after a curious mideastern supper of black strips of lamb and some mushy stuff that wasn't rice and a dish that must have been a sort of spinach. He stared blinkingly across the candlelit table in the drafty hall, where every now and then a wave of heat from the hearth would blow his way. "Yes, it really puzzles me. Here we are. Here you are, Sam. Not at all in the way we might have imagined we'd be after thirty years. And I've been a loyal employee of the Otto Mill all this while and never doubted I'd go on being one and living in the manager's house and raising my kids and staying happy with Ann. And here we are with you, down here in the woods, having a time like old times, and I'm not feeling a traitor for it. I'm feeling instead like something is changing here, in the village. Not because they're trying to take it away from us — that's what I used to be afraid of — but that we ourselves could almost take it all back." "Too much to drink, Pete," said Ann, raising one eyebrow owlishly.

"Take it all back?" said the quietest dinner guest, Otis Cable, moody and vaguely depressed, as he'd seemed all evening, seldom glancing at Sam but slyly observing the shy Qatari who brought the dishes to the table, passed them round, returned to the makeshift kitchen and, only after being severely importuned, sat down modestly on the bench at the end of the table beside Ed, who had overindulged himself and was now nodding and snuffling. "I meant take it all back for ourselves the way it was," said Peter, focusing afar, some faded photograph from childhood, possibly, glinting before his eyes.

"But it has never been ours," said Otis. Khaled, uncertain, turned his flashing eyes on the glum man up the table. What sadness lay in those syllables? He had caught the word "never" — Khaled knew that one, a sad sad word, a word that haunted him, too — never to return, never to see again, never to touch or hold all the long lost past a wide world away. He thought these things in his native tongue, of course, but the English word "never" was mingled there.

"Yes," said Peter, slowly drawing out the vowel, stretching his stomach, heaving a heavy breath. He was jowly, Peter, his features losing themselves in a doughy face atop a slackening neck. "Because before Ottos, it was Thornes," he admitted. "It was always somebody else. But the valley itself — lord, Otis, you should feel it more than any of us — once wasn't anybody's at all. It waited here for us." "So," said Ann, "how about draining it out now, Pete? Let the dam go. Otis Pond is leaving *you*!" Witty Ann. "And flooding the hell out of me down here," said Sam, who'd been staying out of this, a curious sparkle beneath his lowered lashes. "No, no, no, no, no, no, no . . ." Seven stuttered noes from Peter. "I meant something much simpler."

Now bleary Ed Forgan came to from his little snooze and released a massive belch, ignored by Otis and the Dokes, but Sam gestured for Khaled to pour him another glass of the port they'd switched to. "Stop," said Ed when the dark liquid was about to spill over. "What are you god damn ass holes yapping about now?" (Discrete syllables in the swears, the mark of Ed Forgan.)

"My husband wants to take back the town from the Ottos." "Annie!" "Oh, sure you do, Pete, we've been living under the brow of that hill far too long." "Annie!" Domestic stalemate. Everyone knew Ann was the smarter,

Peter the dreamier; if the times had been more advanced, she would have been running the Ottos' mill for them and Peter working the looms. Ann had hard edges and a view to fresh results; still, Peter, as he was, suited his employer fine. They trusted each other. No faint hint of discontent or unrest had ever been discerned by either through years of smooth sailing: Peter as the village's representative to Mr. Otto, Mr. Doke as Fred's spokesman to the village. Take it back from Fred? Unthinkable, until a quarter of a drunken hour ago when wine — and this precise configuration of old friends — had allowed Peter a thought that had lain long unclaimed, the thought that Frederick Otto, Jr., had no more right to what he had than Peter did. It was a revolutionary thought, but a thought at the heart of American thinking, desperately though we strive to convince ourselves that we've all been offered the same fair chance. This subversive thought, left unexpressed, drives us further into our lonesome selves, despising our failures and adoring *their* grandeur, sitting on hilltops where once any flock might have grazed or gazed moonward pondering the peaceful vale. And, see, Peter stepped back from this thought, too, and joked at Ann as she joshed him. ("Haven't you heard, Pete? Socialism went out last year!") He, too, let go the misty notion: they had their jobs, they had their house until they retired on quite a reasonable pension, most of all they had their children whom they knew how to love, and no one knew any better thing on earth than that.

Sam Lara, however, was something else again. No realist, nor sentimentalist either. "Let's get Ed good and drunk," he whispered when a thoughtful silence had fallen, "he's not nearly drunk enough yet." "I have never," said Ed, "been drunk enough. I think I'll go off for a drive. I'm not too drunk to drive my trunk. Funk. Fuck. Truck. My truck. I'll go fuck something in my trunk. Truck."

Khaled was giggling now. These silly white-skinned people, when will they ever be left to thirst on desert sand or starve on a blighted plain? When will fire rain on them from the sky, blood flow in their rivers, and where will they hide then? And why do they strike me so funny? The one sip (or, truthfully, it was three sips) of wine on my tongue, could that alone have rendered everything so foolish? Look at Ed, the first crazy one of them I ever saw, the wild man with his truck bounding over the ruts and potholes, that word he keeps saying — I know "truck" but I mean the word that rhymes with it, the word Sam himself sometimes shouts out when he is making love with me, the word he has sometimes moaned in his sleep. These English words are so abrupt. And now Sam, my Sam, pouring himself more wine, and more for his drunken old friend . . .

Who can say if these were the thoughts of young Khaled? He could not be divined as the others could.

When the party broke up, it was the soberer guests who set off up the road together, leaving two mad dervishes behind in the care of the staid foreigner. Luckily, the truck — the village's truck — was parked up on the plaza. Small likelihood of Ed taking it for a ride in search of four-letter words; he could scarcely even stagger home without supposing a nice nap in a snowbank might be just the ticket. Meanwhile, the Dokes had invited Otis Cable in to warm up with a cup of camomile before trudging on home to bed.

One entered the manager's house, the old farmhouse in which William Otto had hatched all his enterprises, through the el, the door between woodshed and tack room, and wended one's way down a narrow passage to a creaky stair and up into the kitchen with its dark low-sagging beams and great iron cookstove, warming ovens built in above and a mantelpiece cluttered with the handiwork of children: miniature canoes of birch bark; a mitten rack decorated with nearly identical masked green faces belonging apparently to four individual Ninjas; an untenanted out-of-kilter birdhouse; a lumpy clay bird enameled brilliantly blue; a wreath or a crown or a basket or a — well, something made of pinecones; and behind it all a child-drawn calendar with February's sleds careening down the white paper between spindly trees, scarves trailing from the necks of their gaping-mouthed riders.

Peter stoked up the fire and set the water to boil. There was an electric stove in one corner, which he eschewed in winter. Otis took a seat at the long table in the center of the room, a regular trough of a table, where the kids would line up on one side to face their provident parents whose aching backs rightfully claimed the fire side. The children's seats were, Otis found, just a trifle small. He felt the same sensation of his largeness he had experienced on a visit to the village schoolhouse some years back for an assembly honoring Miss Griffin on her retirement, all her old students there for one final admonitory lesson. She lay in the graveyard now, but then she still had things to teach long-winded Mac Rhodes (from her very first class), to teach her little lovebirds Peter and Ann, still to try to teach Ed Forgan — all of them. Naturally, Sam hadn't been there, and Otis had missed him acutely. It was a premonition of the return, Otis now realized, the memory of Sam more persistent in that classroom than anywhere else in the village; that was where he had had Sam under scrutiny five or six hours a day. School had been filled with Sam, every moment of it.

That small plateau past the plaza before the hill leads up to where the Thornes and Laras once lived, that only truly flat part of town where the school and the church and the parish house and Dr. Henrikson's old house were, that was a region Otis had usually avoided in his adult years. Sam still hovered there in the schoolyard, the scarier Sam, also on the Aldridges' old front porch where he had sat with Sunny one whole summer while Otis spied at them gloomily as he laid brick for the doctor's new front steps and walk.

All these memories from merely applying my bottom to this narrow chair! thought Otis. Ann was back from checking on the kids. The eldest, named for *our* Rosemarie, had put her sister and brothers to bed and done her homework and not watched TV and left a lengthy note to that effect.

"And so, Otis, town meeting's coming up," said Peter, pouring from kettle to pot. "Assessments. Now *there's* something we can take a stand on. Ann already put the bee in my bonnet. I'd be the perfect one to propose the changes since we're given this house and don't stand to gain anything ourselves. Besides, Fred agrees something has to be done to level things out. Look what those Januses are paying, and those headshrinkers! There's no relation to the prices they paid for their houses. And, Otis, you're shelling out too much for a house you paid off the piddling mortgage on decades ago. It didn't cost your folks but three grand to

buy that place." "A little late in the evening for high fi-
nance," said Ann, sitting down beside her mate. They both
sat taller than Otis in his stumpy chair. "Hi, Mom and
Dad," he said with a chuckle. "It might be dicey, though,
if Sam got in on our politics," Peter went on, determined
to have a discussion.

"This is what Pete does," said Ann confidentially to Otis.
"We have a roaring good time out without the kids for
once, and then when it's bedtime he's all revved up and
wants to reorganize the world." And so her husband directed himself exclusively to Otis as well: "Believe me,
Otis, it's Ann who really wants a little upheaval. You know
what she thinks of Carol Otto and her chummy little drop-
ins down here and how carefully I'm always smoothing
things out without any help from my old agitator here."
"Old agitator," murmured Ann into her tea. She was a
scrawny, angular woman having never lost her angular girlish scrawniness. Her humor was so wry you weren't quite
sure it was there. But it was. Sometimes, Otis thought, it
might be the only thing that was there for sure, the rest of
Ann the hollow reed she resembled.

"The real question," she stated, still under her voice, "is
where does Fred's loyalty lie. Is it the newcomers he really
cares for, or is it us?" "Ann used to be a defender of Fred,"
Peter pointed out, as if she wasn't even in the room. "She
said he gave us a better deal than in many a union shop.
She even liked his damn retirement apartments. But these
Tarnoff-Rice people and Bodmans and even those professors
babbling along, they do get her goat." "That Janus woman's
a menace," said Ann. "She wanted to have a glimpse of
the old Otto house, she said. I told her it's been a hundred

years since any Ottos lived here, so she wasn't about to find their geegaws lying about, that stuff's all up the hill, I told her. You like to see the beautiful calendar Rosey made? So I made her suffer through it, month by month, and all the time she's peeking around absorbing the history — that's what she said she loved about Otis Pond, all the history she now calls hers!''

And so the talk had descended into gossip, the nervous system of any village. These newcomers! The older Troyer son, the serious one, Barrett, had been told not to back his pickup into the Blairs' driveway when he was plowing snow. He'd offered to plow them out for free; he needed the maneuvering room if he was to clear off the schoolyard. But those friendless people in the old parish house put a chain across their driveway instead. And the Tarnoff-Rices were just as angry because he wasn't up at their place plowing them out the minute the snow fell. What if there'd been an emergency! they caviled. Well, who did those people think they were? And those snotty kids of theirs in Mac Rhodes's store — Kathee Thompson had told Ann she was ready to poison their Dove bars.

Otis finished his tea. "Well, I guess we aren't going to solve the world's problems tonight." Peter was trying to conceal his yawn, and Ann was fairly propping up her eyelids. When Otis finally emerged from the Dokes' back door, he cast his sleepy eyes past the barn where Fred and Carol garaged their Dodges up the long driveway to the big house where no light shone, then along the pond road toward the plaza with its single streetlamp. Somewhere out in the snowy land, Ed was swaggering and staggering. When Peter switched off the light in his kitchen, Otis found himself in the dark whiteness of a winter midnight. Strange illusion — everything beneath him white as white and yet all plunged in blackness. When else do you experience the two colorless shades so impossibly coextensive? — no alternating contrast like the black and white linoleum tiles of his own kitchen floor, no blending into the grays of his woolen sweater, but rather two constant presences, pervasive, simultaneous, as though each, translucent, were filling the very same space before Otis's eyes.

The camomile had not entirely sobered him, he realized. What then? Something was drawing him up the back street instead of home by the pond road — the memories that had assaulted him earlier, the sense of the long ago summer, with mosquitoes and bees, him kneeling in the carefully graded sand, slowly setting brick next to brick, peering between the hedges across the street at Sam and Sunny necking? Necking! A lost word come back to sting him again.

His footsteps led him there. All dark. Ann was right: there was now a heavy chain drooping between the granite gateposts of the old parish house. Opposite, the computer people's front walk, Otis's brick path, was nicely shoveled. (Had Barrett found another client? Barrett, who worked for the county road crew but kept himself busy after hours janitoring the school and plowing or mowing as the season demanded . . .) Otis remembered when he was a boy being brought to Dr. Henrikson's for inoculations. Mrs. Henrikson had let him sit in her parlor, even after the needle, let him pull books out of the shelves, any ones he wanted, and read in the warm lamplight. They had books not found in the village library, big books of paintings and drawings and works of more recent literature than Frederick Otto, Sr., had yet admitted into his public collection of classics: Willa Cather (who was buried over in Jaffrey, Mrs. Henrikson had told him — a wondrous fact for young Otis to find himself that close to a real author) and John Steinbeck and Frederic Prokosch — so real and so imagined — all these she let him borrow if he returned them carefully to her mailbox, which of course he faithfully did. But he read as much as he could sitting there in the doctor's parlor, his arm already knotting in pain from the shots. Mrs. Henrikson used to bring him cookies — marvelous afternoons, irregularly dotting the calendar of his youthful years.

Now, cold and dark, he crept up the brick walk — the Bodmans wouldn't hear him in their sleep — and there he crouched, turned — yes, here it was, the same vista, the front porch across the street, not the Blairs' now but the Aldridges' again, the lovers entangled there as only teenagers can entangle themselves. And a mosquito buzzing at his ear . . .

No, what was that summer sound? A creaking, a squeaking. Was this his dream or something in the February night? Otis stood. It was coming from the other side of the doctor's house. He stepped back onto the sand-strewn street and walked, crunching, toward the noise, which had a steady beat to it, like swinging. At the back corner of the schoolyard, by the Henriksons' laundry lines, the rings were in motion. A slim figure dangled there, legs too long but twisting awkwardly to keep aboveground as its long arms reached from ring to ring, no little monkey but truly an orangutan, hoary and ceremonious in its airborne journey up and back the five cold steel rings on their squealing chains. It was Sam, it was drunken Sam, it had to be Sam.

Otis crouched again behind the jungle gym, slight cam-
ouflage but still a kind of protection, bars from behind
which to watch a great ape.

But what was he actually seeing? Was it maybe young
Sam again, already too tall for kids' things, already interested in girls and cars and beer but still driven by those
hands of his, those arms, to grasp, and swing, and thrust,
and punch and pummel, to kick with his legs and stomp
with his feet, to burst out of everything, slam, pound, run,
leap, and swing and swing and keep swinging? What rushed
through his simian mind at a time like this? No thoughts
of the meditative Otissy sorts but stark principles: get,
grab, have, take, go, leave, break . . . He was fitted for the
desperate game, marked out for others' hatred as he swung
there. An orangutan from an East Indian isle beset by man
and destiny but, even at bay, inured to hunters: they'd have
to kill him, they could not merely snare him. Up and down.
As long as he moved!

The swinging dark shape was hypnotizing Otis, whose
gloved hands, one above the other, clung to the iron bars.
Yes, Sam would take it all back. Peter's words at dinner
had pricked him. He and Ed had gone on to drink themselves into an ecstasy while cautious Otis and the married
folk had headed safely home. But Ed's ecstasy was of the
baser type and foul and off he'd stumbled to wallow and
collapse, while Sam's was ethereal, transcendent — no
Otto could capture him here in his old schoolyard where
once he reigned. The entire village lay asleep while he was
swinging, lulled by the pervading power, the aura spreading
from the monkey rings, soaring across the night to blanket
us.

VI

At the last moment, Joanie's presence had been desired in Keene or she would have been at Sam's as well. Ann Doke had been expecting the additional feminine presence, not that she minded particularly finding herself alone amongst the men. Strange sorts of men these were anyway to spend an evening with, she concluded; it scarcely seemed to matter to any of them but Peter that she was a woman. Otis, as always, was indifferent to her gender, and now it appeared Sam was, too. And that strangely girlish Khaled — how uncomfortable he made her, so pretty and delicate and unmanly — he seemed drawn to neither sex. On the other hand, Ed was drawn to everything indiscriminately, but to sex itself rather than the participants. Well, it was largely a village of good solid families, so these few anomalies naturally grouped together. Admittedly, their company was sometimes a little livelier than the Troyers or Thompsons or Grandys — iconoclastic, amusing, not so damned settled. But when was the last time Ann had dined with Ed and Otis in a formal way? Years went by in the village with old friends seeing each other daily — over coffee or lunch or just in the street or at work — but never sitting down to supper together at home. Another effect of Sam's return, these gatherings of a purely social nature — Ann rather liked them. Why had the villagers always relied on brown-bag lunches for shared repasts? Why couldn't we do as the gentlefolk on the hill did? And whatever might result from the Dokes presuming to invite the Ottos down for a family meal? Perhaps, that was the truly revolutionary gesture in need of being made.

Still, it seemed a little overwhelming, to live as the Januses or Bodmans did, reciprocating dinner parties, keeping parlors presentable at all times, larders full, an ample liquor supply. No, the coffee mug and teacup were the natural vessels of social exchange in Otis Pond. All one needed to make a friendly move was a boiling kettle and perhaps a plate of cookies. Then there were those men who preferred their beer. We all spent so much time working, after all — the boring quotidian expenditure of body and mind on tasks with slight reward on the spiritual plane. Getting along, getting by, keeping up, keeping at it — there it was. Thank you, Sam, for your hospitality, but don't expect us to carry it further. We're tired. So how about a hot cup of tea and a sit by the fire late some chilly afternoon? That's all we have to offer, Ann decided.

When she went to the post office the next day, she reported on the evening's intrigue and prepared her old friend Joanie for a bit of excitement at town meeting next month. The two women promised to sit with each other, and when Sunny came in for a money order she joined their conspiracy. It was still fun for these three to club together as they had as girls, when Rosemarie Troyer made the fourth, a seamless little quartet. For all the boys did to annoy or distract them, they always found refuge in the whisperings and stifled giggles of their confidences. Nothing, finally, could undermine that — except time, and even time could not dispel the impulse to revert, on occasion, to their close-held intimacies. And nothing brought forth that impulse more readily than civic events when the little boys of their youth took on the roles of town fathers. Serious as the issues at hand might be, there was always something riotously funny about Peter Doke and Bill Troyer and Dick Reichardt or, lord knows, Otis Cable or Ed Forgan speaking up just like Mac Rhodes or even Fred Otto himself. Mrs. Paulson, who considered Mac and Fred her younger brother's set, had confessed once to Joanie and Ann that she couldn't take her own generation seriously either. "Frankly, girls," she said, "it's not so much the perspective of age. It's just something about them being men. The best-kept secret in the universe is that men are actually rather silly. Don't tell my daughter. Her marriage is rocky enough already." "But, Mrs. Paulson," said Joanie, "you always took Sam seriously." "Seriously? Oh, I don't know. But I have a soft spot for Sam. That's what it's really about, dears, I suppose — soft spots. Their silliness, our soft spots. Besides, you can generally get all you need out of them if you know how to tickle them just right." "You're definitely the power-behind-the-throne sort, Mrs. P," Joanie had remarked.

And now, with Sunny (another, if somewhat more obvious, practitioner of the Paulsonian art), Joanie and Ann dived into a disquisition on the nature of sexual love. What Joanie had to contribute, from the state of her current affair, was welcomed by her pals in a way, she later told Otis, she didn't imagine married men would welcome corresponding notions of his; men certainly haven't any great urge to get at the nuances — at least not in words, that was Joanie's impression. Otis allowed as how she was probably right, in most cases. And Joanie made a further claim: men of the usual sort are terrible storytellers — they're either windbags like Mac Rhodes or, like Sam Lara, they don't let on a thing. Otis found himself nodding in dreary agreement. "But I'll find out Sam's story, Joanie," he said, "if I have to live to be ninety."

Joanie doubted his success. What she, Ann and Sunny had concluded, with rhapsodic Sunny leading the way, was that at the very core of love — for another, from another — resided a necessary secret still point, an eyelet, an emptiness almost, a blank space not to be filled, a tale left untold. What do we ever *not* say to Peter, to Chris, to Dick? What do we not quite ever say to ourselves? Where does it lie hidden? Isn't it in that same place from which our laughter springs? And don't our whispers blow all around it like vivifying breezes? In some small place inside you, Joanie, are not Ann and Sunny also alive — as we are in church singing praises to God the Father while in our silent hearts we know it's an all-embracing mother we're creating right there in that crowded room through our song, our shouts, our stomps and whoops? Too philosophical a speech for Sunny? Well, this is a mere word-bound approximation of the communion evident in the post office one lunch hour amongst three old comrades, as different from one another as pinecones and green apples and strawberries. If only Rosemarie, long since transplanted to Massachusetts, could have brought her spicy self along, too!

The Ottos returned from Sanibel Island, their Florida

escape hatch, laden with seashells and seared with suntans of the old-fashioned leathery sort, in time for the March town meeting, which in the event proved to be anything but a diverting evening, even for the female contingent.

As soon as she'd shut the post office that afternoon, Joanie had begun organizing the tax records, one of her peripheral duties as sole concierge of the village hall. Why hadn't she done it earlier? She'd known the meeting would require an up-to-date report, but she'd put it off and talked to her friends and mused over what other commemoratives to order along with the Elvis issue and even spent more than her allotted time studying offers for swaps from fellow philatelists — letters, magazines, obsessive little brochures that came in her mail . . . Ed had pulled up in the truck and set about opening the hall upstairs. He replaced a bulb or two, unboarded the windows, pulled the old sheets off the desks and chairs in front and began setting out the folding wooden seats in irregularly Ed-like rows. Joanie brought up her electric space heater to take the chill off and made sure Ed did a little sweeping.

The room was larger than any in the Otto house, but its ceiling was sensibly lower. Stairs at one end led down to Joanie's domain and up to the vacant offices and storerooms of busier days. The hall itself was used with declining frequency. An itinerant lecturer might speak on Transcendental Meditation or Libertarianism, but the Ottos no longer sponsored the monthly series, which in decades past had imported such attractions as a marginally famous poet, a mycologist with horrific tales of death by fungus, a missionary lady and gent showing their gorgeous color slides of Tahiti and Rarotonga, and (if memory serves) a "futurist" forecasting personal computers in every home and a TV recorder capable of showing any film you wanted in the comfort of your living room. In that same hall, Franklin Otto's consort of viols had performed ad nauseam, and Mac Rhodes had tried over several widely spaced seasons to organize amateur theatricals with such aging plays as *Separate Tables* and *The Constant Wife*, disastrous evenings for actors and audience alike.

When the villagers began venturing up from the entrance on the plaza and once again caught in their nostrils that musty woody scent of the old hall, each must have renewed a private memory of an evening passed there: embarrassed, bored, heartened, angered, inspired. By the time Peter Doke struck the gavel, fully fifty citizens had gathered. In the front row of comfortable seats sat the oldest generation, shaky old Daddy Griffin, rickety Mrs. Grandy, Sr., the Collins patriarch, and Judy Nelson from the kitchens of Otto. Behind them were Fred and Carol, separated from Sam Lara by the earnest Bodmans, and the Januses sat eagerly right behind. Dick Reichardt had beckoned Sunny in beside them, but she made impatient gestures to indicate he should realize she'd rather sit with her girlfriends. Ann and Joanie were across the aisle in front of Otis Cable; Ann's sharp elbow was nudging Joanie to notice some drollery on the other side of the room.

As she took the next seat, Sunny, not to appear too exclusive, turned around to greet Otis — the first time they'd really spoken since that rather intense evening two months earlier at Joanie's. "You know, Otie," she said, reviving a nickname from his earliest years, "I was just thinking about you this morning. I had to write it down then and there. Here, see?" She unfolded a scrap of paper from her parka pocket and waved it at him. "It was in this inspirational literature I picked up at my church. The epitaph or whatever it's called, you know, at the start of a book — a Herman Melville quote. See?" Sunny's book, apparently, was something called *A New Age in the Nineties* by Drs. Bewick and Brown, licensed psychotherapists. Otis read the words they attributed to Melville: "We dream not ourselves, but the thing within us." "Very inspirational, Sunny. It happens I'm about to begin reading *Moby-Dick* again, my third time." "See, Otie, I knew I saw one of those Herman Melville books under your arm at the store last week. You must've read every book in that library three times by now." "Some," Otis admitted. "Most!" Sunny proclaimed (as she thought) flatteringly. Otis gave a shrug inside his layered sweaters. "It's an epigraph you put at the start of a book, Sunny, not an epitaph. You put an epitaph at the end of a life." Sunny made her oh-stupid-me face and, before turning away, said, "No, you keep it," when Otis proferred her the paper scrap. It would give him something to meditate on during the painful hour to come.

Just before Peter's gavel fell, the silent Khaled slipped in on the other side of Sunny. Why had he not come with Sam or Sam saved him a spot? The women turned left to inspect the newcomer in their row of four. Well, at least he wouldn't try to comprehend their secretive asides. Sunny offered him a brief and rather blank closed-lip smile. Ann nodded. Joanie merely peered along the row. Khaled, with a delicate motion of self-effacement, slender fingers (the littlest one with its bright golden ring) brushing shyly across his inclined profile, eyes downcast, seemed to be asking pardon for his very presence. Amongst women? In his country was it even permissible to accommodate himself there? And shouldn't they all be veiled and behind some protective screen anyway? Strange adaptations necessary in the New Hampshire hills. But how little he seemed a man anyway. That faint hint of mustache, viewed close up as Sunny did, amounted to little more than what on a white woman would be merest peach fuzz. But everything about him was dark and threw darker shadows; his lashes, his brow, his hands, even his lips — nothing rosy in young Khaled, no hues of a northern spring such as were emerging in the faces of Emmy Grandy and Kathee Thompson sitting across the room with the Troyer boys. Whack went the gavel, startling Sunny who received a sudden poke from Ann and a knowing glare in the direction of raggedy Ed Forgan standing on the far side, his eyes carefully positioned above Kathee's tightly stretched ski sweater.

Town meeting came to order. Peter was good at this sort of thing, Ann had to admit. Odd as it was to see him presiding over his elders and betters, and perversely tempting as it was to superimpose on the picture of a sturdy town moderator with a necktie under his sweater her private vision of that same good citizen stark naked rolling about with her and nothing but moonlight on snow illuminating their bed, Ann felt a certain pride of attachment alongside her affectionate condescension. Was this the convergence of impulses from which girlish giggles sprang? This strange synchrony of marvel and absurdity — how else can one love? Sunny had been circling around the same thought in that great lunch hour confab of theirs, hadn't she? Even Joanie, deviant though she was, had seemed to grasp it. It must be particularly a woman's notion, thought Ann. And wasn't it similar to the way she used to tickle her own firstborn, little Rosemarie, that gurgling adorable blob that was all hers?

Now Mr. Bodman was speaking — something about how he could make a program to handle all the village's financial records and he'd gladly donate time on his computer for the treasurer, or whoever, to keep the books. Like his wife, he was a serious hearty sort; they both could be seen — at all hours and in any weather — in matching sky blue running suits puffing up the county road and back, her mass of hair flaming orange, his cut close, redder and darker. Everyone was murmuring appreciatively at his offer, but Peter Doke seemed to think it a matter best worked out between the keeper of records herself and our generous new neighbor. Keeping her own counsel, Joanie determined she would never have to learn Bodman's system.

The tender topic of property tax assessments was ready to be broached, but Mr. Fred Otto asked if he might briefly have the floor first. He liked to keep the village informed of his current thinking. After all, whatever decisions he made resonated throughout Otis Pond, even to the families not directly employed at his mill. The business of sail-cloth — well, clearly it wasn't precisely for sails anymore that the stuff was produced. Indeed, except for a limited number of "historical" utilizations, no one had much need for the material to sail boats anymore. The village, taking the temperature of his mood, began a tentative chortle along with Fred. We all know, he went on (in words more numerous than Ann or Joanie or certainly Sunny allowed to register on their consciousnesses), that in our times sailcloth has come to be used primarily as a designer fabric, for handbags or hats or slacks or curtains or cushions. It attracts rather an upscale market. They make nice billfolds out of sailcloth. Very popular down in Florida. It's a texture people respond warmly to, full of associations, rugged, enduring, intrepid, dashing, maybe even a little rakish. Fred paused for a solitary laugh that had quavered up from the row of oldsters in front of him. What he was trying to convey, he assured the meeting, was that there was a future for the mill if we took stock of our markets better. "As it is, ninety-three percent of what we produce goes to non-nautical usage. I am even now," Fred declared, "negotiating a couple of new contracts with some fellows I've come to know on Sanibel that will keep us afloat well into the next century. But," he conceded, "along with new targets a certain amount of streamlining is unavoidable. As earnings improve, production facilities can be upgraded and that will, in turn, contribute to further growth. There will be no layoffs, I can pledge you that." (This last sentence registered precisely on the women's eardrums.) "But I shall rely on attrition to scale us down. It seems unlikely that new positions will become available in the foreseeable future . . . or the unforeseeable future," he added a bit sheepishly and sat down. Ann could see Carol patting his hand.

The room lay still. Peter rose to thank his boss for his candor. "We've always been able to trust Mr. Otto to tell us as much as he knows as soon as he knows it," Peter said in an unshaking voice, "and that keeps us all honest, doesn't it!" The laughter now was pro forma and a little nervous. "And I think we may count our blessings," Peter went on, causing Ann to gulp, sending him an extrasensory message with all her soul to stop before the mood turned sour. But he wasn't receiving her. "Other places, a good deal larger than ours, have been going under these days. We suffered a big loss a dozen years ago when Mr. Lara died. Still, his executors were prudent in closing the down-stream mill. It was painful for us at the time, but it allowed the village to focus our energies upstream where we have surer prospects." Stop, Peter, please, stop. Don't you see Sam sitting there before you lowering like a thunderhead? And there's Sunny smiling her smug little smile at baffled Khaled who smiles politely back. All Ann could do was grab Joanie's hand for a fearful squeeze. Joanie's face seemed to mirror her own worry. "It may come as a disappointment to those of us who had hoped our kids might find work where we've all been so happily employed . . ."

"Give it up, Pete!" shouted Sam. "Out you go with your tail between your legs! Skedaddle!" He had risen to his feet. The fluttering of the crowd turned quickly to bluster. "Back off!" yelled Mrs. Paulson's son-in-law — at Sam? at Peter? Who was on whose side? Peter tried to gavel the meeting to order. But Sam was still standing, too, and speechifying above the din. "Fred Otto is not the boss of this village. This village is not his mill. This village is the people in this room and a few other loafers besides. That's really all it is. Fred's mill is only an attribute. It sits on the banks of the Quidnapunxet . . ." More people had begun to pay attention. An attribute? Some attribute, though. What was Sam Lara carrying on about? Mrs. Paulson, however, had put on her doting mother expression, and Joanie could see a sly smirk quivering at the edges of Ann's thin lips. Something lively was under way. Sunny seemed to have been set virtually aglow, a strange dazzle in her eyes, and beyond her, Khaled sat rigid, ready to leap to his master's side if need be, neither proud nor worried (how could he know what was at stake?) but alert to any signal of distress. Joanie didn't know what she herself looked like — a blank stare was all she could manage. "That mill, it sits there like a prison, like a pasha's fortress. I've been in prisons like that, chums. I've even landed in our own county jail a few times, remember? But here I am, free, and so are you, free from Fred Otto's upscaling and his designer fabrics and his honest lies." Fred, now standing again as well, had assumed an air appropriate for a doctor on a mental ward. If Sam thought him a mere attribute then Fred must remain all the more unshakable, all the more real, the actual object, the mill itself, the bulwark against the feverish tempest roaring his direction.

The three women in the fifth row on the left weren't saying anything, but all around them whispers still rose, eyes darted. "He's a vapor," Sam was shouting now. "He's an illusion. His money is a paper shield. Has he ever heard of a strike? Reforming the tax structure isn't the half of it. What? Generous Mr. Bodman here is going to pay five percent more while penniless Mr. Cable back there gets a three percent cut? That's all you hope for?" "Sam, this isn't the order of business," said Peter, having laid his gavel down and relying on old friendship. "You let Fred speak, Peter, you let him gobble along in that language he picked up somewhere in Florida — utilizations, streamlining, attrition. That's not Otis Pond language, Fred. We call it 'your profit.' We call it 'firing us.' Whose village is this, Fred?" A scattered constituency had started to applaud. To egg

Sam on or drown him out? Ed Forgan was laughing loud and long and spouting, "Yep! Go to it! God damn!"

Not having quite worked out what she would say, Joanie found herself on her feet with words coming out, soft but quickly turning louder, then very loud, to reach Sam and Fred and that bobbing row of white heads between them and Peter. "Break it up now, boys!" she was hollering. "Break it up! Come on, now! Enough!" But this was fun; Ed was right. She sat down but screamed all the louder. Pat and Susan Janus kept twisting their heads around not to miss a thing. "Let him have his say, Peter," Fred was confidently demanding. "Let him talk as long as people have the patience to listen. I shut up an accuser of his once. I made my mistake and won't make it again. Let him talk. Let everyone talk. You all know who I am. But do you know Sam? Does anyone know Sam? Did Jim Ezzelino know Sam? Perhaps he did. What's this about a prison, Sammy? Where was this prison? Or a seraglio, was it, Sammy? Something fierce as hell must've happened there for Jim Ezzelino to come at you like that. He'd hardly risk his own shameful secrets unless — " Sam burst back with "Aw, what secrets could a character like that even have, Fred? That he prowls around lovers' lanes and watches dirty films?" Ed Forgan whooped at that. "Fred, he's just another upstanding member of the Chamber of Commerce with a little hobby. What's your hobby, Fred?"

More disconnected applause punctuated the general babble. Peter sat down, much to Ann's relief. His boss had told him, after all, to let the scene play itself out. He decided to peruse the tax rolls Joanie had handed him before the meeting, look busy, look unconcerned — wisely, Ann concluded, for it caused the pressure to drop off. The mill owners' voices were still agitating the air but more like sails luffing as a wind dies. The political moment, such as it was, had ceded its place to a personal duel. Isn't it always that way? Ann thought. She turned to Joanie. "Sam's enjoying civics as much as he used to enjoy delinquency." "He couldn't tell the difference," whispered Joanie, not sure she'd heard Ann right. "Uh-oh, look." She elbowed Ann's rib and nodded toward Sunny, who was starting to tremble, tears right at the edges of her eyelids. Now Sunny's going to stand up and say something, Joanie realized, but she couldn't (and Ann wouldn't) pull their friend back down. "Listen to Sam, everyone, why don't you listen to Sam?" Sunny was saying, with just enough poutishness to capture the attention of those around her. Sam glanced her direction. Dick shot up from his seat and crossed the aisle but not (as Joanie first feared) to silence his wife. Instead, he grabbed her hand, raised it and yelled, "Yeah! What good's a couple of percent to us?" Sunny: "Right! Where does that get us!" Dick: "The newcomers are putting thousands into their houses. They're living like we never dreamed of living." Sunny: "They can afford twenty percent!" Dick: "Twenty-five!"

What had Sam and Fred been railing about a moment ago? That the one had god damn better not besmirch the other one's character because the other would start besmirching the character of the first one as it had never been besmirched before, and what *had* happened to Jim Ezzelino anyway, and wasn't it time to have it all out? Where was Sam when he should've been in bed? Well, where exactly was Fred, for that matter? What the hell difference does that make? You ask me, I'll ask you. Whose word . . . But by then, Sunny and Dick had captured the floor. And now the Otis Pond town meeting wasn't quite what it had ever been before. Shane and Barrett Troyer were on their feet chanting, "Twenty-five! Twenty-five!" and the Januses were looking suddenly anxious, the Bodmans stony. Who knows what the Tarnoff-Rices would have looked like, but they were not in residence on weekdays; they had, no doubt, mental wards of their own to attend to. And the Blairs, as usual, were probably barricaded in the old parish house, as indifferent to village politics as to villagers; they got their thrills from daily infusions of gothic fiction.

The little village hall was ringing. Joanie had to cover her ears. Ann crept by her and along the wall to the front to stand by Peter's side. He'd taken the gavel in hand again but was hesitating. Carol was clutching Fred tightly, their faces as brown as tropical islanders' in a cold white place. Only one other such face gleamed darkly five rows back, an alert sentinel, waiting. Sam was ignoring the percentages that bombarded the echoing walls and kept his tirade aimed solely at Fred. Ann had heard, as had everyone else, of the boss's dizzy spells. In psychic concert, she and Carol were warding off the next one, for despite everything Ann couldn't bear to watch Fred collapse. And how would it help Sam? He was no assassin, at least not on our shores — she hoped; she hoped along with the suspicious village that Sam wasn't worse than he seemed, than he'd ever seemed. But was he maybe a little crazy? What he kept spewing in Fred's direction, it wasn't to save the village, surely. It was Sam being only Sam, Sam alone, Sam on fire. "You dare to assume my heritage! How do you know what resources I have at my disposal? Why do you think I won't gear up the

Lara mill again? A village cooperative, a family enterprise, a real family. . . . Do you have any idea how much money I brought back from Ophir and Sheba and Cathay?" Fred was looking a little stunned. Sam loved to bluff, but could Fred ever bluff back at such a pitch? In Ann's brain — in Carol's, too — shone the picture of a fine old house crumbling in ruins atop a hill, the vines on its slopes creeping higher in profusion, wrapping it round, commencing a slow strangulation.

And now, in the reality of the moment, daughter Sue, having put on more weight (NordicTrack and StairMaster notwithstanding), was pushing her way to the front of the room to stand with her father. The time had come for Khaled to move to Sam's side. There he went. Joanie felt suddenly alone — Sam and Khaled, Fred and Sue and Carol, Sunny and Dick, Ann and Peter — she turned to look for Otis, who was staring at a piece of paper in his rough hands. It's a bad moment for him, thought Joanie. If it's anyone's village, it's his. If he loves anything, it's us, Fred and Sam alike, and me, of course. This village is inside him. It's the thing he knows, in every corner of his soul. I know it, too, but I'm the deliverer, the linker, the net — he's the undercurrent, he's down inside. He could say something, but he won't. He has the power to walk up there and stare right into the eyes of Sam and into the eyes of Fred and bring them to silence. But he won't. Maybe he thinks this is all his dream, but he doesn't wake up screaming from it, he doesn't fall in a faint. He lets it swirl. Some deep stream pulses on through it, the old stream in its old channel, where dams and mills and looms and spindles are all unknown.

"Otis," Joanie said, waking him, "maybe we should just

go on home?" He blinked and raised his head and nodded. Fred Otto was now speaking the very words he, Fred, had been wanting to speak in public ever since the year began. "Riches from the East my foot!" he crowed. "You're a blasted murderer as far as I can tell. And who will say you aren't?"

Tumult. Sam's haughtiest laugh soaring above all, but his eyes shot furtively to the sixth and last row, to where penniless Otis Cable had sat, but he was gone.

VII

In mud season the village is at its worst. But if you're a villager, it hardly matters when grime gets tracked across floors, when crisp air has turned soupy and the blue skies take on a gray that's not steely, not ashen, but spongily gray, sodden right through to the ionosphere. Because the change has its promises: puddles mirroring the murk lie scattered in the woods like the steel pennies of Fred Otto's childhood, when copper was saved for the war.

This little war of his own now was a cold one, and he was cold, colder than he'd ever been. In the depth of winter, he'd never felt such a chill jabbing at him as now on an April afternoon. His walk took him, lonesomely, about the village. Everyone was still at work, working for him or working in some capacity that sustained the well-being of his establishment. Otis Cable, for instance, was engaged in rewiring the school building, which had been found to be dangerously below code, as a state inspector had put it. And Barrett Troyer — that sour young man who'd shouted percentages at town meeting alongside his renegade brother Shane (whom Fred would've liked to fire on the spot, but didn't, couldn't) — Barrett was assisting Otis, neither of them on Fred's payroll, exactly, but wasn't everything done for the village a matter of Fred's support? A donation had seemed in order in memory of Miss Delargy (news of whose death in San Diego had reached him only that week); there would be safer, brighter lights tomorrow.

Fred had circumnavigated his domestic enclave and was passing up the gravel road, where cascades of mud had descended the rills eroding the slope. He approached the graveyard. Here, at this spot, Sam Lara had once barred his passage. No Sam was there now. He had not seen Sam since town meeting, but what he remembered best, in all the shouting, was still the sight of that young Arab, his white parka unzipped and hanging loose about his frail torso, stepping through the villagers to Sam's side and how Sam had laid his white hand on the other's brown one and how the younger man didn't tremble in such an hour as that but, with silent lips and (Fred clutched at his own chest as he imagined it now) a heart scarcely beating, his eyes proclaiming to Sam that even if all his recently regained friends should flee his side, even if all his followers should turn against him, we — Khaled and Sam — we will not part, and I will say farewell to life before I part from you. Unspoken, but there, in an instant, for Fred to comprehend, too. Could one man love another so? Isn't the loyalty of wife and child the greater thing, and hadn't Fred felt his there at his own side? So why did the picture of Sam and his — what? — his lover make his heart ache like this? It certainly wasn't any buried impulse of the flesh that lay unanswered in Fred's psyche, but something lay there nagging him nonetheless, the notion of having such a friend, such a fellow. His son Franklin had never been such for him, no more than Fred had for his own father. Mac Rhodes, Peter Doke, Gault, Murray, his Dartmouth roommate McKinney — no presence stood beside Fred now in the graveyard where the snow had all but seeped away and the granite stones tipped here and there a millimeter farther, after one more ferocious winter of their perpetual watch.

Fred made it to the crest of the little hill beside the birch tree. He read the legend on Sam's ancestor's tomb — "I am small and despised . . ." Why must men stand beside other men to know that their hearts are sound? Funny, Fred thought, I've almost felt the steadiest beside Otis Cable. In some words or other, in some easygoing way, in some distracted moment, I should let Otis know that.

The surface of the pond was breaking, and only the thinnest shards of ice still gloomed near the banks beneath the watery skin. The entire volume of water was again applying itself to the turbines of the dam where, all winter, only the artery that never froze had been pressing in concentration through its channel, rendered invisible by ice sheet and snow blanket.

Snowdrops and purple crocuses were peeking out of the mud beneath the column above Gerald Lara's grave. You old monster, thought Fred, but he went over and touched the monument with his cold fingers. Where may I go now? he wondered. Where else in my village? I'll as surely end up here anyway as those Ottos down there who came before me.

He rejoined the gravel road inclining to the plaza and looked for the low oval stone denoting Mrs. Cable's resting place. LUCILLE, it read, deeply etched. No further word, no date, but there it was. Her husband's stone, beyond in the shade of a hemlock, still bore a crust of ice. The winking other eye. Many still remembered these two, more her than him, perhaps. Apparently, she'd drowned. Fred had been unable to say a thing to Otis beyond firmly gripping his hand at the church and squeezing at his shoulder, for a mere moment, with all his might. Carol had written and Fred signed the note as well. And there had been a donation to the church.

Christ! gasped Fred aloud on the muddy roadside, and tears nearly came to his eyes. So many twinges like this lately. So lost within himself. Poetry! he found himself saying — poetry! And he rushed on to the little library. Every book that mattered to him he already owned himself, but here were the copies he and his father and his grandfather — or, more truthfully, Carol and his mother but not his grandmother, his grand*father* — had bought for the village. It may have been quirky restricting the collection so, but experience elsewhere surely would bear out the tendency of designated classics to fade into the background when engulfed by shiny new books with splendid dust jackets and up-to-date titles. Sadly, William Otto's cultural experiment had run its course and now found itself powerless to entice the newest generation; Fred acknowledged this. Still, to stand there in that little room, docked (as it seemed) at the edge of the pond, was to feel ever eager to set sail anew. And these words shall launch me, thought Fred. But before he crossed the room to find his Blake or Coleridge, to begin chanting their invocations to the silent shelves, to the windowpanes, to the opaque grayness of the pond, to the muddy hills and shivering trees, he stepped to Mrs. Collins's desk and scanned the latest borrowers' page.

So his Sue had been plowing through the set of Willa Cather in pale green bindings, which were among the books Mrs. Henrikson had presented to the library some years back when the doctor died and she moved to a smaller house in Keene. *My Mortal Enemy, A Lost Lady* — titles familiar but unsettling to Fred. Were they as grim as they sounded? Sue needed something more cheerful. Ah, the ever-present Januses — Dickinson and Poe this time. Mrs. Collins had told Fred she suspected Susan Janus just came in to chat — it was always during the librarian's hours and any book would do to justify her visit; she certainly had her own shelf of standard poets at home.

Odd, Otis hadn't been in for some days, but no, there was B. Troyer with *In Dubious Battle* signed out in the blue strokes of what surely was Otis's sober hand. An unlikely protegé, Barrett. Bitter, disrespectful. If you must convert the heathen, Otis, better try the more responsive and cheerful Shane, though Emmy already has his heart. But can I ever forgive those boys? Or the damn Reichardts. . . . And what's this, in faint pencil below?

Lara,   S. Whitman, W.   Leaves of Grass

But what will that man make of "Out of the Cradle Endlessly Rocking"? Fred felt the need to clutch again at his own chest, to still the beating — the thought of Sam, dread Sam, despised Sam reading a poem that, for no reason he could ever quite capture, always made Fred gulp back tears. That thought of a possible communion he and Sam could never now share was shaking at Fred's innards. If they had only read such a poem together a month ago — rather, if they had, thirty years back, read it, talked, walked — no path would ever again have been barred between them.

His hand at his breast touched the pocket there. And then Fred remembered what he'd carried about with him for several days, the summons to a hearing, which he, in lieu of any designated village constable, was authorized to serve on Samuel Thorne Lara, River Road, Otis Pond. He kept forgetting he had it.

Where was Blake? He needed a prophecy. He needed to shout something aloud to the empty library where he and no one else had ever raised a voice. But that was the mill bell sounding across the plaza. Work is over. The village will flood into the street, the children screaming out from Sunny Reichardt's day care (Fred's innovation, yes, *Fred's*), and the older ones will gallop down from the schoolyard; the impromptu soccer match will scrape and scuff across the gravel — ah, there's Shane Troyer already and his future brother-in-law the Grandy boy. Ploff! goes the ball into the air — and Joanie Voshell at the post office door. . . . Should Fred emerge, too? Could he now? Would anyone even notice him at all? Or he could slip off through the graveyard, back the way he'd come.

As he huffed up the steep shortcut to his kitchen entrance, he heard shouts from the plaza below. The village sounded happy as ever, even if it wasn't. Perhaps it was because the first whiff of gentle spring was blowing off the melting pond, the mossy rocks, the pine needles. Fred's boots were splashed with mud. He removed them and padded stocking-footed into Judy's kitchen. "Good afternoon," she chanted merrily, rolling out dough for the pecan pie Sue had been yearning for. "I was standing over your old friend Lucille Cable's grave just now," Fred said, surprised at himself for the confidence, modified as it was. "And I found tears coming to my eyes." Judy looked up. "I didn't know you ever thought that much of her," she said, squinting warily. "Oh, I suppose it's because of Otis," Fred offered. "My own mother died so much more comfortably; Otis had such a run of the worst things happening." "Otis is fond of you," said Judy. "I think I know that," said pensive Fred. "Besides," Judy went on, a pallor crossing her puffy cheeks, "Lucille was going down faster than anyone could hold her back. I'm speaking of her drinking, Mr. Otto. Now, see, I don't ever intend to go like that. And I ain't the retirement type. You've got me for life, and I'm making it a long one."

Carol had come down with the day's washing in an ample wicker basket. She set it by the laundry room door when she noticed Fred's squishy socks. "I'll take those," she said. "Your slippers are over by the stairs." "Ah," Fred sighed, cozying his toes in the fur linings. "I'm awfully well taken care of."

Later, when Carol came back down again to put the sheets in the dryer, the baking pie, having sent wisps of aroma up two staircases, was luring Sue close behind her. As her mother hummed over the wash, Sue carefully assembled a tray of smoked oysters on toothpicks to carry up to Dad in his study. But the man himself was now descending again as well. The three women were startled to see he was not in his homey sweater and jeans but was accoutred like the businessman he was — his Chamber of Commerce outfit, even to the overcoat and briefcase and rubbers over black shoes.

"All right, it's time," he said. "I can't put it off." "You're going to Sam's?" "If I'm going to do it, I have to do it, Carol. I can't live with this damn summons forever in my pocket. Besides, that was the state police fellow who just called. They've got computers that trace these things. Some trooper in Arizona remembered about that MANGIA license plate. He saw it nailed above the counter of a truck stop in Flagstaff. They think it could be some sort of clue." "Jim's alive and well and living in a pueblo?" Carol proposed. Fred shrugged. "I don't suppose Sam's ever had anything to do with the Southwest. He was off roaming other deserts." Carol asked if, in his heart of hearts, Fred didn't really just want Sam entirely off the hook, vindicated and under no further suspicion. "I think all I want," Fred said, lifting the car keys from the bowl on the counter, "is to find out what Ezzelino had against him. Why did I ever think I didn't want to know?"

"Be careful, Daddy," Sue said, "I'm sure Sam Lara has a gun. Or at least a knife." Then she giggled and passed him an oyster. "Mangia!" she declared in somewhat doubtful taste. Fred held up his palm at her — no. "One for the road, Daddy!" All right — he curled his fingers down to pluck up a morsel by its toothpick and pop it between his teeth, then laid the wooden splinter back on Sue's platter. At the door Carol said, "Maybe he'll agree to show up in Keene, Fred. With all his petitions and unionizing and arm-twisting, maybe he'll welcome an opportunity for some more rabble-rousing. And he's certainly no stranger to that courthouse!" "Fix me a nice tall old-fashioned for when I get back, Carol," Fred said and kissed her cheek, then headed down the drive to the old barn and backed out his Dodge. He caught sight of Otis farther out the pond road heading home from the schoolhouse job. Fred turned right and passed the wiry Barrett Troyer in his engineer boots stomping along toward the plaza. The young man's head didn't turn.

Fred's Dodge was nearly twenty years old (Carol's was younger). Cars meant little to either of them; they traveled seldom and when they did it was by plane from Keene's small airport. So their cars were rare presences. They didn't make the edgy whine of Japanese compacts or the hum of the newcomers' larger imports, nor did they roar like the trucks and vans favored by most villagers. The domestic old Dodges glided so silently that practically all you heard was gravel crunching.

The soccer players dribbled over toward the bridge once they sensed the blue-gray Dodge nosing eastward. It crept across the plaza, deferring to Lila Doke and Patricia Grandy who skipped randomly back and forth. Why hadn't he gone the back street way to avoid this awkwardness? No one seemed to see him at the wheel. He felt encased in silence. But when only the tail of his car presented itself to the plaza, then all eyes turned and watched and wondered as Mr. Otto descended the river road to the old Lara mill. That way where else could he be going?

VIII

For barely a graspable handful of minutes, the village was stilled. It would reanimate itself when the two men who held it in thrall (or one of them) returned to tell the tale, but now a lethargy settled over all, heavy like the spongy sky, like the wet bricks of the mill; there was heaviness in the feet of the resting soccer players, of the children who'd just been skipping about, in Barrett Troyer's boots as he eased himself down and stretched his legs out on the village hall steps, scarcely nodding to Joanie Voshell who leaned exhausted against the post office door-jamb, the air almost too thick to breathe.

The river ran, after such rains, but what other sound was there? No wind to rustle the trees. Tiny drips from the hall's leaky gutters spattered at Barrett's feet. That was all. He saw his baby brother holding the soccer ball sitting on the bridge abutment beneath that corny sign — "WE'RE NOT!" Mac Rhodes's brilliant idea. Had to push it through town meeting. And there sat Mac on his store steps with Kathee — Kathee, who kept bugging Barrett when she should've got the point by now. They were waiting, too. Everyone was. Subdued, Lila and little Patricia were poking sticks around in the gravel at the edge of the mill parking lot. Mrs. Reichardt and her second daughter Marian were watching over them. Marian was Barrett's age. They'd been a graduating class of their own, and now she was studying at Keene State to be a teacher. She'll never leave home, though, she'll never get married, Barrett figured. It was Gwennie Paulson and that crazy Puzzo kid from the road crew who were the first of Barrett's bunch to get married, with Shane and Emmy coming up fast.

The sleep-dreaming little village in front of Barrett's eyes seemed smaller than ever. Mac wasn't gabbing. Kathee might sit there forever, until maybe a delivery man made off with her. That's how it all felt. How did we get here? Those two men down the river shouting at each other — if that's all they're doing — they keep us here, both of them. And one other man. That seemed an odd thing to Barrett. It felt as if Otis kept them there — well, maybe not all of them, but him, Barrett, at least. Otis hadn't taken a side in all the uproar. He wouldn't sign Dick Reichardt's tax petition. He wouldn't talk with the union representative Sam Lara had brought in to stir things up. But he certainly wasn't standing with those newcomers in the big houses either. He told Tarnoff-Rice he wouldn't repair his screen porch. He'd stopped serving at the Ottos' dinner parties — even if they'd only had the one since town meeting. Otis Cable was on his own private strike, Barrett guessed. He would only work for the village itself — rewiring the school, mending the church roof, helping Ed patch potholes. And he'd have to be getting to those gutters over Barrett's head. And repointing the library bricks. And all in that quietness of his.

Barrett realized it wasn't the confrontation down the

river that was making him so sleepy now. It was what Otis
Cable had been telling him after work. Barrett's Aunt Rosemarie had talked about it to him and Shane some months
back, what the village figured went on between Otis and
Sam when they were kids. Barrett had tried not to think
about it then, but Shane had actually once asked Otis
straight out; Shane had the kind of nerve, or was it just
stupidity, that never failed to stun Barrett, who had to go
through life excusing his brother. Still, it was all something
Barrett himself did want to know, too. And there they'd
been, working together all day, Otis in the school basement
passing electric cable through holes in the floor and snak-
ing it up to Barrett in the junior room fishing around to
pull it up from below. Only voices and hands. And the
junior and senior classes combined going on in the other
room so the men could get the job done, Mrs. Thompson
shushing everyone.

And after work, it had felt somehow easy to lean with
Otis against the jungle gym and take one of the beers from
Otis's cooler and hold on to the slow quiet mood. Even
years later, after they'd become partners for life, they would
recall that same feeling whenever it was an April day and,
looking out from their kitchen table at the melting pond,
something about the light trapped in the clouds seemed so
familiar from a season long past. And the way the setting
sun eventually pierced the horizon and lit the top of the
ridge where the cut of the county road curved up and
over — then all the past stood witness before them again.
Barrett would remember how, before the mill owners' wild
ride began when he was sitting there on the village hall
steps with what Otis had just been telling him pressing on

his mind like a mud slide, he'd felt for sure the first touch of a thing already growing up inside him, his passion, his devotion, and he'd remember his amazement that Otis Cable would have begun to tell him, just Barrett, his temporary assistant, no one special, what he had never quite told anyone, what even Joanie had never fully known or Landes cared to know: how Otis and Sam had all so briefly become lovers in the high late-summer grass along the river.

To give his tale a beginning, Otis had to go back all the way to an October encounter in the graveyard when, having meandered about after school in his ten-year-old aimless way, he'd come upon Sam, also dreamy and aimless, leaning against a gravestone. And Otis had found himself not quite so trapped in the serious silent side of his nature as he was at school when Sam would ask him about homework or call him names. He'd showed off a little — what he knew about the village, the land before the village — because Sam had asked him questions, but their voices hung stiller in the air, time was slower around them, and that fearful rough edge of Sam's seemed softened, like a smoothly planed board in his father's shop. Sam hadn't seemed to be resisting Otis's company. Even when he dismissed, in his typically ornery way, the very notion of history, of looking back at things, Sam remained receptive, regretful, and perhaps almost mournful, as Otis had never seen him. A ten-year-old boy with tears in his eyes — not from cuffs and scrapes and punches on the schoolyard but from a thought — that must have been the moment their compact had been silently made.

These encounters recurred, almost as if prearranged,

throughout the year under Miss Delargy. Otis might sense that Sam was sitting on the bank across the bridge where ice was forming, or climbing in the snowy woods at the end of the pond road, or strolling down past his grand-father's mill along the river road's rutty far reaches in muddy spring. And Otis would find him and they would talk, or not talk but think and look and even once in late spring plunge into the rushing river modestly in their un-derpants. If he said nothing about it to anyone, Otis knew they could continue to conduct a private friendship. But in school, he still had to hear Sam jab at him with "you queer" and "you spaz" just as Sam called Ed Forgan "pree-vert" and "ree-tard" and Joanie "Chunkie."

Their secret meetings must have numbered barely a dozen, but with all else now evaporated from that distant year, Otis remembered them as numberless. He was always either in anxious anticipation of the next crossing of their paths or in the shimmering afterglow of the last one. If when Sam went off to boarding school their relations changed, and if Sam seemed no longer to need him as his touchstone, he hadn't forgotten him either. So by twelve, they began what would have seemed to a grown-up a pre-maturely retrospective phase of the friendship. Otis now was Sam's past, Sam's childhood, rendered irretrievable but nevertheless still acknowledged. Who knows but that Sam, at school, spoke to his new pals about a best friend in his hometown, a kid who was actually part Indian, a kid who knew everything about history and literature and who would do a lot better at such a fancy school than Sam ever could but whose father was just the village handyman and whose mother was a drunk — and without ever having to meet this Cable kid and be disappointed in the mundane original of Sam's idealized portrait, his school friends could help him in casting a spell against homesickness, the fact of an Otis, bolstering Sam in his lonely dormitory, something to lean back musing upon.

In summers or vacations, in the weeks Sam wasn't sent off to camp or to visit a new friend in the suburbs of Boston or New York City, he roamed the village as before, and the path-crossings occurred, if infrequently, but never again in the old mood. No lingering, no peaceful silence, but a quick exchange of news ("Oh, nothing much" always began it, but something of import, or at least interest, would eventually emerge) and then a few remember when's and sometimes a penetrating sort of curious stare from Sam that Otis couldn't fathom, until it dawned on him it might have something to do with the same erotic impulse he himself had been cautiously exploring in the darkness of his attic bedroom. Was Sam searching for some indication — that Otis was doing it, too? And if Sam was, what then? What did it mean?

On a summer afternoon when they were thirteen, Sam had got drunk on a big bottle of beer he'd lifted from Mac's store. He'd kept it cool in one of the falls of the upper river, way in the woods above the Cable house. Otis had seen him sneaking around up there at lunchtime and, when he'd finished helping his dad by meticulously cleaning and reattaching the carburetor on the Collins Ford, he wandered off up the hill, too, with a book (*Crime and Punishment*) under his arm to mask his intent. He found Sam easily enough where he was sunning himself without a stitch on.

The Quidnapunxet before it reaches the pond is a picturesque stream, but few bother to acquaint themselves with it. It tumbles between stony banks in a deep bed and pours exuberantly over boulders and ledges, whose higher shelves provide sun and supreme privacy, and the roar deafens the ear to any intruder. At a distance, Otis could have safely withdrawn, or he could even have stood and watched Sam lying back like a naked Indian on a flat rock with water bubbling where his feet dangled into an eddy — like a *drunken* Indian, more likely, with that tall bottle nearly polished off. But Otis, fully clothed as always, with grease-stained hands and grease all over his jeans, found himself witlessly approaching until Sam sensed movement in the trees, let out a great hoot and told Otis to come join the party.

Sam's body had matured, as Otis's had, but it didn't seem to trouble him to have Otis near him on that rock. Otis supposed boarding school boys spent all sorts of time naked together; he himself hadn't been naked with a single other soul since his toddling days. Barrett got to feeling a little uneasier when the story reached this point and kept staring into his beer can, as if he could actually see something inside down there. Luckily, Otis didn't carry it much further. He left it that two boys — three dozen long years ago — did the same things boys might still be doing except they didn't have to call it anything back then. It was merely delight. It arose naturally. And you couldn't get girls to do it with you quite yet, anyway, though Sam did have certain female prospects in view, he assured Otis afterward. That didn't prevent him from also proposing a rematch the next afternoon, however. And so it went for the months of summer.

"But, Otis," Barrett said, a little unsure of his ground, "you said you became lovers, and that isn't what I'd call being lovers exactly. That's just, well, like you said, kids fooling around." "No, that came later," Otis told him, "that was later and darker."

So Barrett set down his beer and hooked his elbows back around a bar of the jungle gym and ventured to look, maybe for the first time, into Otis's suddenly serious face. He could hear the shouts from the soccer game on the plaza and a few piercing little-girl screeches from afar.

Otis began by recalling one Christmas vacation when Sam was hanging around his mother's with nothing much to do, probably wishing he was back at school where his real life was now. At the sight of Otis Cable heaving shovelfuls of snow off the Paulsons' walk next door, he decided to ask him over. When Otis learned that Mrs. Lara had gone to Keene for the day, the intimation that he might be about to find himself in a real bed with the companion of his soul shot such excitement through him he was sure Sam would sense it and back off. Nothing should ever be too feverish around Sam; Sam had to be the fevered one, but physically so, ambitiously impulsively wildly, and you had to follow and submit and admire and never expect or require or demand a thing. So Otis trembled as he stepped into the kitchen he'd seen before only when helping his father install Mrs. Lara's new stove and trembled some more as he watched Sam pour him a beer from the fridge — his mother knew he took an occasional beer, Sam claimed. And then he followed Sam up the back stairs where he'd only imagined what it must be like, into a bedroom strewn with tangled dirty clothes and lacrosse equipment — an old Indian game, Sam informed him. There was a shelf of model cars, a hitherto unmentioned hobby, which Otis inspected and praised. But something cold was in the room with them, too. What might have been a bed of love was, as it soon turned out, more like an exercise mat. As such, it served its pleasurable purpose but left Otis feeling lonely and expendable quickly enough. And he was dismissed before Mrs. Lara came home. Sam didn't have to say she wouldn't like the idea of him having Otis Cable over because Otis understood it instinctively, as he always had in their friendship, whether it was of Sam's mother or the kids at school or indeed of anyone in the village at all.

So he withdrew and found himself launched upon a terrible couple of years; his father's illness meant Otis had to take over the tasks that kept so many village folks in such good repair, and it meant his eventual retreat from education and from his heretofore more sociable self. He would still talk to his neighbor Joanie. But if there was anyone he ended up spending time with, it was likely to be Ed Forgan, the most boring kid his age, the two of them crawling under some chassis or leaning into some engine, to earn a few bucks from less mechanically minded villagers.

Then came the summer of Sunny Aldridge — that's how he designated it for Barrett — the worst summer of Otis's young life. Sam was surely gone from him at last. The increasingly unrealistic daydream that accompanied him everywhere, sustaining and depriving him in equal measure, was turned now into an absurdity. And yet, Sam was even vivider, more alluring than he had ever been. His energies had spiraled into something more frantic, needing to have everything that was to be had and the very same instant refusing it. Consequences now were considerable: no broken windows or charred diving floats, no pilfered snacks and beer bottles, but high-speed smashups and undesired pregnancies. His mother didn't know what to do or say or even think. She worried Sam constantly, but when she talked once, ever so hesitantly, to her father-in-law, he only blamed Sam on her Finnish blood. A stalwart Yankee with a strong admixture of Spanish pride would never behave so maniacally. Why his son had ever married a Finn and then gone and died so soon, Gerald Lara would never know, but corralling his young ruffian wasn't the business of the patriarch, even if Sam was his sole heir. Sam had not been invited to his grandfather's table in some years, yet the old man must have envisioned his future reform and Sam being all the stronger for the length of time it took in coming — or else he wouldn't have so carefully provided him with such a considerable trust. Did Sam already know about that? With safe haven, did he simply do whatever he damn well pleased? Assuming he survived, he'd at least never have to go begging.

Otis watched Sam throughout that last wild summer and, against his better sense, was more in love than before. "But why the hell?" spat Barrett, surprised at himself. "I mean, Sam was obviously a total asshole!" and Otis couldn't really answer him. "It must have been something in me instead," he finally proposed, "some yearning I didn't understand." And Otis still didn't understand it; he could only accept it as having been the case, as having happened, as being still alive in him somewhere even then, perennially blooming despite Landes, despite those who'd preceded Landes. "It just seems so weird," Barrett said in almost a whisper, but Otis only smiled and told him, point-edly, that maybe someday Barrett would see for himself.

That summer when they were eighteen, Otis and Sam had spoken seldom — a nod along the back street on the way to Sunny's or browsing in the village store's cooler for a tonic. But, strangely, Sam gave him that searching look of his, once when Otis was going into the library, once again when he was painting old Mr. Lara's back fence. It was a look that said, I know there's something inside you and it's something I think I may want but I'm not about to say what it is, I'm just going to look at you this way and see if you'll break, if you'll put it in some manner of words, if you'll offer it to me. The more wrapped up he got in Sunny's arms — and the arms of some hot ticket he'd met at the roadhouse where the mall would someday be built, and maybe the arms of some older lady in Keene as well (village rumors, spread by Mac and Pop Nelson and Mrs. Collins and even Sam's doting neighbor Dorothy Paul-son) — the more he seemed to be playing the local rakehell, the more he darted those looks at Otis. Signals? What else were they? Otis would sit in the graveyard after supper, hoping the sun would go down quickly and relieve him of yet another day. And if Sam wanted him, where more likely to find him than leaning up against August Thorne's gran-ite stone watching the purple-rippled pond?

Sam did come, one of those evenings. He was downcast. Maybe he was a little drunk. He said he'd been thinking about a lot of things. Too much thinking. A thought isn't real, isn't actual, it isn't like a thing happening, he couldn't ever hold on to a thought. "But *you* can, can't you, Otis?" he'd asked. Otis was scared and hopeful at once and hardly felt like speaking. "I used to," he finally said. Sam must have noticed particularly now what he may have already noticed, in passing, all summer: that Otis was in a kind of trance. It was unsettling. His first intention may have been simply to see if he still had Otis right there sealed up in his pocket as before, maybe not to test it out but just to see, be sure he still held the key. This was a power even Sam had never quite dreamed of. He leaned against the birch, a bit staggered, perhaps — high stakes, higher than the speed of his Mustang on the post road, higher than his head when he was drunk and roaring. And here they were, Otis and Sam, just sitting, like themselves at age ten again. Something frightening came out of Sam's mouth. "You know I love you, Otis."

And the sun was only just setting. It blazed in the tree-tops like a shepherd's fire upon the height, a century past. And now immediately, they were lying in each other's arms, but only for a few seconds, on the grave of Sam's forefather. A reader in the library might have seen them, though of course no one would have been there at that hour other than Otis himself, escaping his rampaging mother. But the little building was dark and Otis was here beside Sam, holding on for dear life and gently sobbing. What would Sam do? They'd walk different ways: Otis as if he were heading home, Sam back to the plaza, past Otto's mill, down the river road, and Otis would circle the other way and across the back street, where Sunny was dutifully helping entertain a visiting clergyman, and then down the cut by the Paulsons' and, down farther in darker woods, they'd meet up by the river. There was a grassy spot where Sam and Sunny went often enough. That was where he would go now with Otis, but Otis mustn't think about it. Sam told his friend what he must do.

Exulting, with all the spirits of the woods and hills and waters singing in his ears, Otis made the slow march. The mosquitoes of the August night be damned, he would bare his flesh to them! They could have him if he could only be with Sam, because he never had really been with Sam yet, whatever those previous foolings had amounted to. But Sam had said it now: the thought was connected finally to the act. Moon, rise! Stars, prink the sky! Oh, heaven on earth! sang Otis to himself, not in words, not in a tune of any sort, but in a single thundering chord such as the church organ made — so loud Otis could always hear it clear across the schoolyard when he was pulling up weeds and clipping bushes on Sunday mornings. And now it rang every treetop, but silently and unheard. The village had disappeared, and Otis was in a virgin woodland. No dam crossed this gleeful river, neither upstream nor down, no pond flooded any meadow, no house had ever been built, no church, no school, no library even (terrible sacrifice!) — just a tiny grassy spot among the trees where his skin would be made to itch, hardening him to what real love was, to its suffering and its hugeness.

Sam was there as he'd said he'd be. He was shirtless. So, soon, was Otis, who then said he wanted not to take off his jeans yet, because it would be better (he was bold enough to tell Sam) if whatever they did came out of something, if it happened because of feelings — no, I don't mean thoughts, Sam, I mean feelings, I mean feelings in my nerve endings, in my body: I want to be taking off my jeans because I can't help it.

Sam seemed to have understood, because he stepped closer and embraced Otis and told him not to be worried. He'd learned a lot since the last time they were together, he said. That penetrating stare again, now in moonlight. Otis was hypnotized nearly. It took few words from Sam — words so welcome, so immediately gulped in by Otis — to make what was happening and their "feelings" seem as one. Sam was telling him how confused he himself had become, how scared he was, too, how he didn't know where his wildness was driving him, how he was afraid he'd have to leave home, that was the only thing he could do, because he couldn't rein himself in anymore. And there was Sam now, actually crying a little in Otis's arms, and then Sam pulling him with him into the long grass in sobs like those gasped in disbelief by Otis in the graveyard. Otis knelt down beside his lifelong friend. Otis held the tearful face close to his own bare chest, stroked slowly the smooth hair, which seemed so long for a boy in those days, and told Sam he didn't have to be afraid, either — he Otis would be faithful whatever happened, he Sam would always be loved. Thus, kneeling, Otis ministered to Sam Lara as he never thought he would have been allowed to do, but for the last time.

Sam was steadier now. Intent. These confessions and pledges seemed to have aroused him even as they had all but blotted mere sex from Otis's heart. Sam straightened up tall on his knees. Behind his head, a thread of gold spun itself out across the darkest blue, almost black sky. One instantaneous filament, then another. It was the time of the Perseid meteors. Here, said Sam, please, take me inside your mouth.

Otis only knew later that it already hadn't been quite what he wanted, it hadn't been quite what should have come next. But he had no experience, and he must have been imagining some rapturous world lying just beyond the first true union now promising itself to him. This was the beginning of the journey there, something would open, no more wrestling and tumbling or beating of hands but a passage to a future he was too young to know about, too constrained within himself to risk discovering — some transcendent unknown place. Slowly he leaned his head forward, down, his bare neck (he could only imagine) dappled in silver light for Sam to contemplate as he raised his body to meet him.

But then Otis felt something laid upon his neck, a cold thing colder than moonlight. "God damn!" came a familiar voice from behind the downstream trees. "Shut up, Ed, he's just about to do it," said Sam. "It's a knife, Cable," said Sam, "it's a knife." "It's a knife, Cable," Ed repeated. "Go on and do it like you were going to," Sam said in the strangest voice Otis had ever heard, a voice that didn't seem to want to say what it was saying. The blade was still cold, and its sharp edge seemed to be seeking the warmth of his blood. "I guess you win," said Ed. "God damn. All right, I'll pay up." Otis was now doing what he was compelled to do, all the time thinking, knowing that Sam was feeling the pleasure of this strange enforced communion. For while Sam's brain was despising him, his body surely wasn't. His body was proof. His body. And Sam's body was Sam. In their secret bodies, he and Sam were making themselves one, still being faithful. But their brains had lied.

And, like a dreamer, for years Otis had continued to tell

himself he had been right. Sam really did want Otis in
some inadmissible way. Joanie always told him she was
sure of it, too, and that made him feel better, even if Otis
had concealed not so much the event as the elusive nuances
from his neighbor. And, naturally, later on, once Sam had
left town, Ed Forgan would say anything; he bad-mouthed
Sam as much as the rest of the village: "Christ, Otis, he
loved every minute of it, that ass hole, course he did. I saw
his fuckin' face. Who was he to call me pree-vert all them
years for Chrissakes!" A myth, an illusion, a plausible excuse for Sam's cruelty remained the mainstay of Otis's
spirit: Sam would have loved him if he'd dared know his
own true self.

And how perfectly confirmed this notion had been, and
yet how wounded, how betrayed Otis had felt (he finally
confessed to Barrett's stricken face) by what he'd understood to be the relationship between Sam and Khaled when
the prodigal returned home with his mate: that Otis *had*
been right about Sam, that this was what he'd gone abroad
to pursue all those years, but that he should have brought
back a slender young man to do what Otis might once have
done so willingly and be what Sam would never now let
Otis be.

"Can I remain so jealous, Barrett?" the older man now
asked the silent younger one. "Or is it a kind of vengeful-
ness I've kept inside so long and all this year, when it's
been hardest? It's mean not to try to care for Sam if I have
the chance, mean of me to stand back from all I've seen
and felt and wished for. Can I ever heal myself of it?"
Barrett's saddened eyes puzzled over the way those monkey
rings there hung still like waiting nooses. He wasn't the

one to answer such questions. So the heaviness came down on both of them. The shrug, the empty stare, the edge of a bitter smile on the lip. They each set off in a different direction, Barrett to find his brother on the plaza — but no, he wouldn't ever tell him what he now knew.

But on the plaza the atmosphere was strange, too. The heavy sky seemed ready to descend on them all. So Barrett sat and waited like everyone else until out of their stupor the villagers roused themselves at the sound of whirring wheels down the river road, and their blank stares focused and Marian Reichardt pulled the Doke and Grandy girls back off the gravel and Shane tossed the soccer ball to Puzzo and hopped quickly off the bridgehead out of harm's way. It was as if the younger people somehow also remembered the times thirty years earlier when Sam would come blasting into town heeding no one and nothing. Mac Rhodes could remember, of course, but he stayed languorously on his steps even while Kathee leapt up to hide behind the screen door. Otis Cable would have sensed the old danger, had he been there, but after he and Barrett had left the schoolyard he'd struck out for home in the opposite direction. But Joanie Voshell, *she* was sensing it; Barrett had caught the recognition in her eye even before the black little jeep plowed into sight, top down, at its full whining speed, kicking up gravel like a wild horse, Sam wrenching at the wheel and Khaled beside him gripping the top of the windshield, head buffeted right and left. At first, the chase produced exhilaration. A hollering went up from the soccer players, safe in the turnout by the library, and then came a collective awestruck intake of breath as they saw what was in pursuit, Fred Otto's big Dodge, gaining as it barreled toward the plaza. Sam cornered tight by Mac's store and swung masterfully onto the bridge where Fred had to take it much slower. What the hell's going on? was all Barrett — or anyone else — could think, except perhaps Joanie who felt more and thought more and feared more. Mac Rhodes just sat openmouthed, storing up the sort of evocative detail he could lard his eyewitness account with so it might serve him well throughout his remaining decades.

What the soccer players saw — they were the first to make it to the bridge — was the tail end of the Dodge flashing red as Fred furiously applied the brakes to stop in time. What Barrett saw, running with Joanie puffing at his heels, was a dab of blackness way up the ridge between some trees. What Kathee saw out the store window on the river side was more distinct: two tiny tires spinning in air at crazy cocked angles. But Mac, from the steps, couldn't make much out with the setting sun hitting his sensitive eyes as he scanned the ridge top. Sunny was running past. "Watch the kids!" she screamed. And Sunny kept screaming, to her daughter Marian, to herself, to the hillside as she ran.

What Otis Cable saw was somewhat sharper. He'd been having a cup of tea at his kitchen table and amusing himself with his binoculars, recognizing specific boulders across the pond and familiar tress. When through his open window with its hint of spring air he heard some commotion afar, he craned his neck up to look higher. He saw it all broadside: the black jeep, open to the clouds above, with two blurry but identifiable figures in it, one small and crouched over, the other waving his hand on high, a kind of take-me-and-be-damned sort of wave to the cloudy big car behind. And then from out behind a clump of trees, the jeep emerged again but it was up on the two far tires only, and instantly — mud slide, pothole, even a lingering ice patch, or just too much speed — it had flipped almost all the way over but was arrested by the muddy bank, and the blue-gray Dodge was jerking to a safe halt. Otis could finally zero in on the silhouette of Fred Otto sitting upright and motionless, but what expression he wore Otis couldn't tell. And the jeep had tipped away from him, shielding its jettisoned riders, its ballast, from his sight.

IX

But what the Bodmans saw, after jogging down the ridge at a clip toward the frightful screeches around the curve and coming upon the overturned vehicle, was first the pale upside-down face, seeming to laugh because of how the mouth hung open, of Sam Lara, blood pouring across his throat, and his left arm flung out and twisted back, seemingly crushed beneath the jeep, and his woolen sweater all mud-covered, and then, as if fallen from above and now struggling back across his crumpled lap, one slender hand snatching at the steering wheel, her white linen shirt rent apart to show smooth brown breasts, the young woman who had played the part of Khaled through three seasons of a northern year.

Up in the tangle of Sam's movable limbs, the foot that had pressed the accelerator quivered. Mrs. Bodman, of the wild red hair, reported later how she suddenly couldn't tell top from bottom seeing familiar persons as if cut apart and pasted together at random. Breathless already from her jog, she feared collapse with dizziness. How could those parts of those people have landed that way? The breasts certainly were extraneous, and where did that blood come from? Her husband steadied her and yelled to Fred Otto, who was finally emerging from his car, behind which resounded the shrieks of an invisible running woman.

Soon enough Fred had ducked back into the driver's seat to motor up beside the accident, and Sunny Reichardt had burst past him, too intent on Sam to notice the transmogrification of his servant. Mr. Bodman and Fred, and Sunny, too, were now extricating the unconscious man from his trap and carrying him carefully to the Dodge's broad back seat to lay him on the lime green vinyl. Khaled — what else to call her? — had managed to stand and stagger to the open door where she took a willful plunge between the men's legs, landing on the car floor, to watch over the one whose life was bleeding fast away.

His head must have been dashed against a boulder when the overturning jeep slid into the bank of the hill. With the scarf she wore she could stanch the blood on his skull: his head had been slammed one way then another, skidding along a granite outcropping. Now Fred was behind the wheel, Sunny beside him, and they were off to Keene leaving the Bodmans, messengers from the world beyond, to tell the village of what had happened and, also, of what had been revealed.

Some hours later, when Fred and Sunny drove back across the bridge, people still waited on steps of store and village hall and library and mill office. Without even slowing down, Fred drove out the pond road right to his old barn to garage his car. Then he strode purposefully up the hill to the arms of Carol and to hold his Sue in his arms, leaving his village to do its best without him.

Sunny was quickly met by the crowd converging outside the Dokes'. She would have to tell it all now. But not yet to Joanie, not to Otis — they had already gone home when Fred's call came in at the store's pay phone and Mac Rhodes had borne the duty of announcing the death of Sam Lara to his fellow citizens. Sunny was hardly ready to speak. Peter brought her inside his gate, and Dick held her, Ann and Peter held them both, while Ed lurked nearby. The rest of the people clustered just beyond the gate, Januses and Bodmans, too. Rosemarie Doke was in tears, but the younger children were simply excited, sensing anticipation in their elders and running about chasing each other amazed to be allowed out so late. The small teenage delegation sat sullenly on the stone wall across the road, assessing events in their desultory way. Kathee, though, had sought out Barrett for comfort, and Emmy clung to Shane. When Sunny Reichardt finally found her voice, then at last she couldn't stop herself. From the first glimpse of Sam mangled on the roadside to his vanished heartbeat when they'd reached the hospital, out it all came. And in the telling, the vision of the unknown woman (so Mrs. Bodman wasn't crazy after all) shone before the villagers' eyes as vividly as did the figure of the dying man.

She, Sunny, had at first not understood what Khaled was, and neither had Fred. But the grieving woman behind the seat, her shirt open, was pressing her lover's silent face to her breast, and in a glance Sunny could see what Mrs. Bodman had seen already. "Sweet Jesus!" she'd said, then hesitated for fear of sending Fred Otto off the pavement. When they came finally to the post road, she answered Fred's "How's he doing?" with a whisper: "Mr. Otto, that

Khaled back there, he's not a man. All this time, he's been a woman underneath!" Fred, madly tense, seemed not to absorb the information. "Never mind that now," he said, "we have to get Sam there safe." And it really wasn't until they were at the emergency entrance and Sam had been wheeled in and Khaled helped by a kind but absolute orderly that Fred could master what Sunny had been trying to convey.

Why, at the moment of utter concentration as death sweeps in on someone we love, do we have to get distracted by such a revelation? If it could have come earlier, giving us time to penetrate the enigma of the real living Sam, ever-elusive friend and foe, or if it could have held off till our grieving had subsided and then produced a comic reshuffling of all our assumptions, in those cases we might have had a lot more to say about it. As it was, we were simply struck dumb. Who dared speculate right then on the proclivities of a dead man? Who would express shock or outrage or, for that matter, relief or amusement? The mysterious stranger, who'd suffered only a few bruises, was sitting up all that night beside her lover — her husband? — in a dark room in the Keene hospital which, but for the cold body there, must have seemed a place where strife could never enter, only silence and peace. *Her* grief was surely unequivocal. She had always known who she was, and Sam had known, so *they* had not been distracted at the moment of death by revelation or astonishment. What must it have been for them to lie in the back of Fred Otto's Dodge? Of all alien places to make their farewells . . .

Once his follower, she was now his guide. Grayness was swirling by above them through the window glass, but they were cradled on sticky lime green vinyl. As Sam's faint breathing waxed lower, the tide of his blood, each convulsion coming in a blacker gush, was now trickling more feebly, though not less fatally. If he moved, it only added another throb to his pain. Khaled gently held the numb and broken hand, wanting so to assuage its pangs, and Sam's mouth only curved sadly now when it meant to offer thanks. But his companion feared nothing, nor felt, nor heeded, nor saw anything but the damp brow she pressed against herself, and she gazed down into that dim eye that held all the light that shone for her on earth. If the man driving them had been their enemy, they were escaping him now, though he still piloted them. They needed say nothing to him. He was forgotten.

At last on the smoother straightaway at a higher speed, Sam did begin to speak, remembering perhaps the exaltation of his youth out on that road, the release from mortality, his bold challenges flung at death. But his words came now in another tongue, which he had never yet heard back then, a language with its own strange memories clinging round it. He spoke most likely of another place, but what he said was known alone to Khaled — let us call her Khaled still, man and woman at once, for the space of Sam's dying — and Khaled replied, though faintly, while Sunny Aldridge Reichardt kept glancing over her shoulder in mute amazement. Those two back there seemed even then to half forget the present. They were in some past, holding up between themselves a separate fate that Sunny couldn't know.

Their murmurings were slow drawn-out throaty sounds moaning through their scarce-moving lips across the short space between them. It might almost have seemed that what impended was young Khaled's death, rather, to hear Sam's voice and breath so sad and deep, so hesitating as the accents broke forth from somewhere lost inside him. At first, his voice, though low, was clear and calm, until death's own murmuring gasped hoarsely nearer, but even then his face seemed unrepentant and passionless, except when his eye could focus on his partner. And then it showed only kindness.

Once, when Khaled's answering had ceased, Sam raised his good right hand a bit and pointed to the East away from which they were speeding. Whether it was sun breaking through clouds and casting its last brightness at the tree-tops behind them that made him think so much time had passed that it was already dawning back there, or whether he was pointing to some memory, to a place they had once been, in response Khaled could only turn away with a heart that abhorred the setting sun. His — her — master's brow would be darkening soon enough. Better he should lose his senses now, before that woman in the front seat mumbled another one of those prayers she seemed to be praying up there. Profanation! No such prayer must touch Sam. She shielded him with her small body as best she could.

Now his limbs began involuntarily to flutter, and his head drooped heavier against her. She pressed the broken hand she held to Sam's heart and with her own hand sensed it no more beating. But she couldn't let the cold grasp go and felt again for the throb that wouldn't answer. Does it beat? Away, you dreamer! Nothing moves inside. You are not even looking at your Lara now. He is gone.

When the car had pulled up by the emergency entrance

and hands out of nowhere seemed to pull her back, up and out from the green glade she rested in, she felt his form no more within her arms and saw the head her breast had sustained lolling on a stretcher retreating from her. She didn't struggle but, released from whatever held her back, she strove to stand and follow but reeled and fell, hardly breathing more than the one she'd loved. "Here, ma'am," came a man's stern voice. "Wrap this around you. There's people here looking." And so, cloaked in the orderly's white jacket, Khaled entered the hospital behind Sunny Reichardt and Frederick Otto, who knew her now even less than they had before. She was alone in the wide world.

X

Over the following days, the controversies that had riled up the village were marvelously set aside. To many, waking with the early April sun, an organized union hardly seemed to have been necessary after all. And surely some compromise could now be reached about the assessments, which would benefit the villagers without driving newcomers off to more hospitable towns. Had we been innocently dreaming of a Golden Age where Otis Pond might sustain itself unchanged in its small splendor? But it had already survived intact a half century longer than it might have. Weren't we, come to think of it now, even a little eager for what else the new times had to offer? Sam had pulled a prank on us, his final prank, but one no more permanent than any other: he had harnessed us to him, he had become all anyone could talk about, he had sat astride us and galloped off on us toward his own last adventure. But didn't we still need Fred Otto as we always had? Even Sam couldn't blind us to our best interests for long. We discovered we still honored Fred, some of us even loved him in a way, for we'd felt a curiously sharp kind of

207 : AN UNTOLD TALE

hurt to see him walking up his hill alone after doing what he'd done, in the end, for Sam. Wouldn't he ever tell us how the desperate chase had come about? Wouldn't he explain it wasn't his fault, that Sam had, as always, snatched destiny by the gullet when Fred had offered him mere due process? Poor legal remedies! But what was a summons, really? What, in his sulk at the unruly village, had Fred imagined would come of hauling Sam Lara into the chief magistrate's office? Some questions might get asked, some suspicions aired, perhaps even some un-founded accusations made, but the mystery of Ezzelino's disappearance would persist, no doubt, without solution. Fred had only been grabbing at some proper means of deal-ing with the man who threatened to unseat him, forgetting that Sam had long ago charted his own route around the proprieties.

The unanswered questions swarmed into the Congre-gational Church with all the village. Despite the thunder-ing organ, they seemed to fill the lofty space above like rumors and whispered louder than the hymns. It had been impossible for the Arab woman to forestall the service because she couldn't put her objections into English. And what rights did she have? Indeed, who was she? Wouldn't her papers, if inspected, contradict her sex? Had she entered our country under a pretense contrived by Sam to aid her flight from injustice — or, more likely, from justice? So she sat at the back of the church, silent, as she had at town meeting. She had entered unbidden and alone, her costume still a man's. With her fierce eyes she strove to damn these Christians and keep back her tears. She would be vigilant still, not over Sam's dead body that lay in that box there but over Sam's secret spirit that resided entirely in her soul. Ezzelino might have told us more about her, or at least about Sam's circumstances when he first enlisted her devotion, but that knowledge had dissipated as thinly as the man who might have told it.

The Reverend Bobby Forrester from across the county line read a simple service such as might have been spoken over August Thorne two hundred years before. Unitarian Fred had asked the Reverend Bobby to restrain his impulse to apostrophize in the contemporary idiom, though Fred supposed as much brimstone as the Congregationalist prayer book allowed would be appropriate for Sam as it never would be for Fred in his own more rational church. In the absence of any other family members — for the Laras, as the Thornes, were now only names on stones — it had been up to Fred, acting village constable, to arrange for everything. And as overseer of the graveyard, he had asked Ed Forgan to dig up there where really only one last new hole could be dug; in the future, villagers would rest farther down toward the pond. Fred had already commissioned the marker; it would bear the succeeding verse from Sam's ancestor's psalm: "Thy righteousness is an everlasting righteousness, and thy law is the truth." Whether this was meant to release Sam beyond the strictures of our small lives here or to seal his condemnation, Fred wasn't sure, but he liked the ambiguity — because it kept haunting him, too — and who would quarrel with a Bible verse?

Fred knew he wasn't to blame for Sam's death. He knew he had only stood his rightful ground. Carol had coddled him. Sue had petted him. He had done what he could. But Otis Cable was still avoiding him and only on the morning

of the funeral would come near to say one quiet thing before
going on his way down the river road, wandering off by
himself instead of coming to church with the rest: Otis
had said he would like to take Sam's place at the hearing
in Keene. "I consider myself summoned," he said. "May I
ride there with you, Mr. Otto?" Fred hadn't even thought
a hearing would occur now, but in that instant he somehow
knew it must.

The pallbearers were Peter, Dick and Mac, and Bill Troyer
and his sons. Otis had demurred, telling Peter Doke it went
against his religion to carry a body inside a box and set it
in earth, and when he heard this, Fred didn't know whether
to honor the notion or feel himself shunned further by one
he'd always counted on. Otis had buried his own father
and mother, after all, and been there to watch the shovelfuls
cover them up. Couldn't he be with Fred now, sanctioning
the moment with his reassuring sense of history's trans-
lucence? Or would Otis, with that young Arab woman,
have rather laid Sam out upon the narrow strip of sand they
called the swimming beach and set him afire?

Fred couldn't banish the vision of Sam's dead body. The
doctor at the hospital had told him when he was filling
out papers that Sam had a scattering of scars dinting his
chest, scars not recent but dating to the summer years of
his life, the lost years between his last spring here and the
fall of his return. If they were glorious scars or guilty ones,
they only told (like the scar across Sam's chin) that somewhere far away Sam's blood had been spilt. What other
histories might that body have hidden within itself while
offering only such hints on the surface? And what was
engraved in his shattered skull, interred that day, never to

sit in candlelight beside a midnight reader to remind him always of something terrible, as another's skull had once done for Sam?

It can come as nothing really more than a footnote, the unsavory piece of news Otis Cable supplied at the county courthouse, because it doesn't explain anything further about Sam. In their ride over, in Carol's Dodge because Fred's seemed now too burdened with fatality, the handyman had little to say, saving it for the constituted authorities, but he was cheerful, as he hadn't been in weeks. May had not yet brought its blackflies or the first mosquitoes, so the freshening woods still beckoned on every side as if to say, "Come out and play in us for this one perfect spell." When they reached the big town, the largest in Otis Cable's restricted experience, he fell into a somber mood, so Fred kept silent, too.

The magistrate's office was flooded in sunlight, which turned the wall of red leather-bound volumes behind his desk into a triumphant banner. The magistrate, an old business acquaintance of Fred's, had called in the county coroner, an officer from the state police and a secretary to join the two men from Otis Pond. None but Fred knew that Otis would have something to tell, so for a time the particulars of the investigation into James Ezzelino's disappearance were reviewed and the exact circumstances of Samuel Lara's death carefully recorded.

In brief: not Sam but, as was to be expected, his servant had come to open the old shipping door. (Fred said nothing to indicate anything untoward about "Khaled"; the immigration service need never know what desert outcast Otis Pond now harbored. It seemed Fred didn't wish to pursue Sam's legacy beyond the grave; his case against him was closed.) Fred had asked for Sam by speaking the one word he knew the young creature understood: "Lara" — but perhaps the piece of paper in his hand sent a warning, or perhaps no such scrap could threaten Sam at all. Perhaps it was like a game of his youth. You come to talk? Well, catch me if you can. I'm faster than you are. I'll show you. I'll make you look the fool. Talk? Argue? Compromise? Agree? Just try and find me!

Out of the recesses of the dark great room, suddenly, charged a wild man, grabbing the Arab's hand and pulling him along (Fred did say "him"). They jumped off the loading dock right into the open jeep before Fred had turned his head or even spoken his summons. Sam was roaring with laughter as he drove off. It took a little backing and filling to set Fred's car to the test. Why had he even bothered? Instinct? Once young Sam had barred his way, and he'd retreated then. Now, the faster he drove, the less thoughtful he became. By the time he'd reached the plaza he wasn't thinking of the spectacle he was affording his workers; he only chased that black thing ahead, taunted by Sam's crazily waving left arm.

But when these facts were known and the reasonable conclusions drawn, and when it was stated once more that this hearing was superfluous and should be regarded as merely a meeting between friends (though the magistrate did appreciate Fred's cooperation), then Fred announced that perhaps Mr. Otis Cable here had a word to add — Fred didn't know what — but he'd wanted to come along and Fred hoped he might supply something useful . . .

"I know why I've kept this to myself." So began the

confession. "It was something shameful, I suppose. I'm just a workman around the village. I do repairs, and maintenance, and help Mr. Otto with his household and the like. My family's been in Otis Pond forever. I live alone, I suppose I should tell you. Except I did tell my neighbor, Joanie Voshell, the postmistress, that I'd gone walking that night late. She could tell you that much. She knows a little about my habits, anyway."

Fred was puzzled by such verbal reticence in Otis. How unlike his usual speech, intelligent and bookish. Was this some enactment of his expected role before the law?

"But I hadn't actually gone walking," Otis went on. "I came back on foot, but I'd gone out in a car. Jim Ezzelino's car, after Mr. Otto's party the night before Christmas Eve. I hear you know about Mr. Ezzelino's habits, if you see what I mean — I mean about his habits and mine. Well, there's that rest area, they call it, out the post road. That's where we went to. I don't think I have to go into that. But we just were in his car awhile and snow was falling. And then he said, 'Let's go into the woods.' There was another car parked by the road there. It was there already when we pulled in, but no one was in it. You know all about that place, what sort of prowling goes on down there. I told Mr. Ezzelino I didn't feel like going back in the woods but he said he wanted to see what was going on. I could stay warm in the car and then he'd drive me home. So he was gone awhile, and then I felt so stupid and bored by all this I decided I'd rather be out in that snow walking myself home. That's the way it is when you go down there. It's not a place you stay long at. It gets sort of miserable. I was quietly sneaking off, but then when I got to the post road where it crosses the Quidnapunxet I heard something rustling below, so I crouched down and watched. It was two men by the river carrying something. It was wrapped in a blanket, it looked like. It seemed to me then I might be watching an actual crime. I couldn't see faces. The men were stepping carefully out on a rock ledge above where the water was rushing in a flume of ice. One held the thing in the blanket. The other lifted a boulder from the bank. I suppose it was about a fifty-pounder. Then the one man tossed the thing he held and the other heaved the stone right onto it, into the water, and it sank away in the dark. I expect it soon went under the ice. It happened quicker than I could really see. And I was a little drunk, I have to say. And tired and depressed as hell about most everything in my life. It had been a bad evening at Mr. Otto's already. I crouched there a little till I heard the two cars in the rest area both start up and got myself behind a bushy hemlock. The Alfa sped right by, and the other car, which I really didn't take any notice of except it had been there the whole time, it came shooting along next. It was just some big American car. So that's all. Except when I walked up the river road back home, I did see a light on in the Lara mill and his jeep was there. And I'm sure he was, too, and his servant, of course. Those men by the river, there's nothing I can tell you about them. They were just two dark shapes down there through the snow."

"The Alfa probably got sold out west, at least the license plate found its way to a truck stop in Flagstaff, Arizona," said the trooper, the one who'd done all that poring over Ezzelino's videos for clues. "Remember that robbery in Peterborough some years back?" he asked the coroner.

"The gas station guy at the self-serve who got his throat slashed? For what, fifty bucks? But things keep coming out of the woods these days." The coroner nodded, the secretary kept up her scribbling, the magistrate sat back wearing a sour expression, but Fred couldn't move or speak. It wasn't from suspicion, for he had believed the story, step by step, as Otis told it. Fred never doubted Otis, nor could he now. Why would Otis tell such a thing if it weren't true? If a body were going to be found in the spring thaw, nothing would've pointed to Otis Cable. He had no need to tell the story. In fact, it could only put him in jeopardy. On that night what surely must have stunned Otis was the narrowness of his own escape. If these highwaymen were after the sports car, they would have killed two as easily as one, two in the utmost vulnerability of a hasty tryst. An awful image to have lodged itself in Fred's mind, but how much more ghastly for Otis, who'd only haphazardly escaped through lethargy or, Fred supposed, sexual satiety. Whatever the circumstance, how barely fortunate! And so Otis was surely stunned, and he must have walked like a man who might well have been dead, treasuring but doubting his life with each step, up past the mill where Sam slept safe. Small wonder the next morning in Fred's study Otis had seemed so unanxious at the prospect of the noontime confrontation he alone knew wouldn't take place. But his calm must have also been the residue of shock.

The magistrate was asking Otis questions now, the secretary writing the answers down. The policeman was sitting up attentive again, but the coroner had just slipped out, perhaps to set a search in motion. And now a sadness began to creep into Fred Otto's mind as he realized that

Otis had known Sam had nothing to fear, that Otis was cast as Sam's secret guardian then, though Sam hadn't known it. His old devotion to Sam had risen and supplanted all the loyalty Fred had counted on. "Excuse me," Fred found himself saying, bolting from his paralysis and stepping out the door into the hall. He mustn't let himself get dizzy again. He must walk, get outside quickly. He fairly hurtled down the stairs and out into the parking lot to breathe fresh and free, and the hint of dizziness passed. He'd done the right thing. Decision, motion, purpose . . . that bench over there.

And when he was seated, regretting the ranks of daffodils in their bed of tanbark, a city idea of garden when they should be blooming scattered across a meadow, then suddenly an entirely different realization rushed into his head. No, of course not! Otis had been Fred's all along, was still Fred's. Otis, who could have cleared the air of Ezzelino and squelched any suspicion of Sam had faithfully guarded his frightful story. Perhaps he feared he'd embarrass himself in telling it, for it *was* shameful in its way, Fred allowed. But Otis's habits, as he called them, were no secret, and he would've been forgiven the indiscretion, given the loneliness of his life, the limits of his opportunities. And what had Otis ever cared for people's opinions anyway? No, he could have told then as well as now. So there could be only one reason, once his shock and horror waned, why he never came to the police, and didn't it prove his unwavering allegiance? Let Sam remain suspect in the public eye and, at the same time, let him forever dread Ezzelino's reappearance — at least until the body was found. And when the body was found, for surely it had swirled into some icy backwater now melting fast in the forest shadows where a fisherman would snag it, then the law would naturally pounce upon Sam. The only possible reason for Otis now to come forward at all was that Sam was no longer able to appreciate his vengeance upon him.

The morning sun delighted Fred, and he was breathing easier. He knew he had a guardian. If Otis still troubled him at all it was only because of his sexual indiscretions. But Otis was honorable, despite that. He had reclaimed his self-esteem from a powerful man who had once (if you believed village gossip) done him considerable emotional harm, but Otis had not allowed his enemy to lie forever under suspicion, now that he was dead. At some risk to himself, he had generously cleared Sam's name even as he had previously fostered the mysterious silence attending it. Sam's craziness had probably come from all that silence around him, and he had kept bellowing out into that silence, but finally he was here alone among speakers of a tongue turned foreign on him. He was not one of us anymore. He'd sought to undo our world, but only Otis Cable had truly known that, Fred decided. Even Peter Doke hadn't recognized it in time. It was Otis, Fred's counselor, whom he could eventually mull all this over with as two reasonable grown men when the turbulence had settled.

The trooper emerged from the courthouse with Fred's somber friend at his side. Otis Cable's presence was now required at the riverbank. A patrol car with another trooper and the coroner in front pulled up, and off they went leaving Fred among the regimented daffodils.

Nothing upon the recovered corpse contradicted Otis's account or incriminated him either. He submitted to many interrogations and kept his sentences simple and consistent, as befitted his stubborn Yankee country ways. From his testimony, the magistrate could have got no idea what a well-read man Otis Cable was, so wholly did he disguise the subtler workings of his mind. Jim Ezzelino's body had suffered damage to the rib cage as if from the impact of a heavy stone, as Otis had reported. The loins bore nine stab wounds from a long knife appallingly still dangling there but washed clean of any damning traces, a plain old kitchen knife to kill a cook.

So a murder was recorded in Otis Pond for the first time, through strictly speaking the rest area was across the post road and belonged to the next town, and the villagers had even more to talk about than they'd had all spring, which had been a good deal too much already.

But one of their number had nothing at all to say. And she was silent still a year later, and a year after that. She never told where she'd come from or why she'd left it behind for wild Sam Lara. Why had she loved him? people wanted to ask and often asked each other when they despaired of fathoming her. And what did her disguise serve — some logical purpose or, as simple thinking had it, a perverse inclination best consigned to an exotic other world forever veiled from us? Why keep asking? We can never know. Our dull eyes never pierced Sam's stern mask, either. With her, wild Sam may have been all gentleness. Lips avow nothing, neither smiles nor kisses nor frowns, that we can be sure of. And no more do words, which must pass through lips. We don't decide on love, we don't construct it. And if we try to, where are we really? Far from love, that's for sure. Whatever bound her to Sam was no common link such as the fainthearted might fasten.

At first we tried to coax her back from her wanderings

out the county road to wail against the stones that had ripped the blood out of him. We didn't think it good for her to linger there. We wanted her to come in for a nice family supper. She would accept our good will, silently, gratefully, but whenever she crossed the river to climb the ridge we soon learned not to follow, for to tear her away from the spot where he fell was to feel the fiery eye of a tigress upon you. If, instead, we left her alone there to waste her weary moments, she would talk idly into the air, her tears finally subsiding, her wailing no longer loud enough to hear back at the bridge. Her sorrowful soul played with his shape before her, addressing it and touching it, and never imagining it quite dead.

And she might also creep into the old barn by the Dokes' and sit inside Fred's Dodge in the backseat, once more to recall Sam's words, his looks, his dying gasp. She had shorn her hair and now, at a distance, looked more boyish than ever. But she kept a long black lock in a pocket of her tunic and would fold and press it upon the lime green vinyl, as if drying Sam's wounds again with it. She would ask him questions in her own language and make up the words with which he answered her. Ed Forgan stumbled on her once in there. He decided she'd gone bats, but he couldn't help remembering when first he'd seen her and imagined right off that she was a girl. Those magic woods she'd roamed in so wonderingly and dazedly were hers now for life, and we would all take care of her. "She's got a thousand and one stories, I bet," Ed said, "but she ain't telling 'em." Apparently, she'd taken him for a ghost, and screamed, and beckoned Sam to fly with her from the backseat of the Dodge and out into the morning where no such scrawny frightful ghosts lingered.

She lived still for a season in the mill and, when it turned cold, in a room above the Thompsons' garage where she kept with her Sam's clothes, his family archives of pictures and papers, the skull and the candlestick, the knife he'd clutched in his midnight spasm. She waited by the swimming beach much of that summer, watching the children, and when they'd gone, as the sun was setting, she'd trace strange characters along the sand. Once, walking down the shore from the library where he'd been reading, Otis Cable came upon her faithful indecipherable scratchings in the crimson light. Years would still pass before she lay buried there beside the pond, leaving her tale untold.

＊   ＊   ＊

But what is a tale and where does it spring from? How deep may I dive toward the truth of it? Having spent my life with books, I am still troubled by these questions. If all I've studied in books and pondered and absorbed myself in has been only an approximation of an illusion, then my life on earth has been lived among ghosts, too. Yet I love this elusive life of mine. Indeed, at my late age, should I live another twenty years I couldn't report more contentedly of how things have turned out, for all the lingering on of past guilt, past fury. Perhaps, there's no greater sense of pleasure than to remember the miserable times from a state of happiness. And the books that still surround me at home teach this lesson in their various ways. I sit by my kitchen window and read and contemplate and know that the terrors of tragedy and the discombobulations of comedy are all there on the page with me and that I am here drawing life from them and living, relic though I may seem. They are no more ghosts than I.

But, again, where does a tale spring from? I thought by writing my own I might find out. What I've recorded has been what I've seen and what I've heard, or later heard tell of, and finally whatever else the honest effort of a straining imagination could produce — all I have to offer. It is my story. By this point, you have come to trust me or you haven't, or perhaps I have eluded you. I will tell you I haven't lied, but maybe it's only that I haven't always known where I've been lying to myself or noticed what I've chosen not to tell. In bringing as much as I have back to the surface of time, I can't be sure there isn't some contour still to be revealed under all the waters of the years, and that it wouldn't bloom once more like a May meadow if the old dam were only dynamited to bits.

We tell our own poor tales our own small ways, and it seems we tell them, when we're not poets singing across centuries, as earnest diarists who would find some comfort for ourselves in the telling. Ed Forgan was always full of ways of looking at things. On his deathbed, he still figured Sam had snuck out and done in Ezzelino himself, with me helping, and that stuff about the license plate just had to do with some lucky car thieves. Ed was all in favor of night mischief, as lurid as he could get it; it made for just the kind of tale he relished. And Sam always was crazy, he'd say, Sam couldn't just have a man or a woman, he had to have every god damn thing at once.

Joanie Voshell, on the other hand — I know she couldn't quite ever lay to rest that specter of a gothic Otis shoving Ezzelino into the icy river to save Sam from calumny. But Joanie couldn't pursue her thought. As soon as it surfaced, she'd quickly push it under with her own comforting logic: that she knew me too well, that her thought embodied only my protective wish but not my act. And yet a curious estrangement set in between Joanie and me. By the time she moved off to Florida, we didn't feel as close as we used to. Maybe it was just that our love lives were finally synchronized. We have a beautiful quilt she made for us, we have her letters and cards, but missives from Joanie and Chris to Otis and Barrett have a slenderer degree of intimacy about them than a morning cup of coffee, just the two of us among cats.

As for Sam, who since his return hadn't really fathomed me at all, what might he have imagined, had he known his enemy was safely encased in ice, a knife in his vitals? Might he have construed it as my secret work, proof of enduring devotion though the decades had run by? I'd demonstrated by that act, he'd speculate, that I'd never been humiliated by Sam at all, that I had, years ago along the moonlit river, dedicated myself to his perpetual service, through love. Might Sam have told himself such a fabulous story? For Sam knew he himself hadn't done the killing and he doubted Ezzelino unassisted would've so conveniently departed this life. Who had dispatched him then? Who else but Otis Cable, whom Sam could now admit he'd always remained peculiarly devoted to despite all? He'd never forgiven himself — he'd even said so. That brief union of ours, with Ed Forgan our gaping witness, had traveled with him unforgotten on all his journeys. And the possibility, the likelihood, even the certainty of my rescuing him now absolved all the sins of his confused and incautious adolescence. I, at least, had forgiven him, I had stayed here to save him. A tale of grace, a redemptive tale, a tale Sam could mull over as he bestirred himself for the good fight, to wrest the village from the likes of Fred Otto and render it to the people, hard workers like Otis Cable and Sunny Aldridge and Bill Troyer's boys, who owned it by right of nativity, not like those Tarnoff-Rice people scuttling off to more civil communities where their sort of doctoring met with the respect they felt it deserved.

But who knows what Sam would've told himself really? He liked tales of high heroism and that's all I have to go by. And what of Sam's own story, the one that died in Ezzelino's mouth, washed out by the Quidnapunxet for all time? Is some substitute still necessary to leave Ezzelino finally on the shelf? Back then, for my own soul's need, I formulated several. I knew how cruel Sam could be and presumed he'd treated Ezzelino in a comparable way, though I was ready to believe he had no particular recollection of it in the vast welter of his wrongdoing: whoremasters and slavers in the sex trade, all the rum customers Sam Lara may have fallen in with, young beauties — girls or boys, white skinned or brown, and a certain Italian gentleman deprived of his chance at the forbidden pleasures he'd come so far in search of. No doubt he had hardly known Sam Lara, had only played an unfortunate but forgettable part in one ruthless episode of Sam's unrestrained career. Whatever it was, it was probably no more a matter of life and death than was the interrupted tryst of our seventeenth summer, no more a life-and-death matter than that overblown civic battle between the Lara and Otto factions. Of such conflicts is vengeance born, but the only forces that held death and life in balance for Sam were Velocity and Play, and the time when Sam would no longer be able to turn aside quickly enough was a thing known only to Manitou.

I've always looked to books for surer stories than I can invent. That cracked-spined volume of Byron rejected by Leota Colburn in her winnowing of imperfect bindings from the now merely decorative Otto collection over there — it's mine for good; with every household grabbing whatever program or piece of information its collective heart might desire out of thin air, it hardly matters that a volume of Byron's oriental tales is absent from the public's complete set. Let me open it — ah: *The Corsair*. No one now is familiar with the famous old story. But here it lies before me, and mightn't I discern in its galloping couplets the possible enormities of Sam's wandering years? In his peregrinations, he too must have left behind any number of sworn enemies — for all I know, that skull belonged to one of them.

But though I'm tempted to read the poem through once more, to absorb it, translate it, reinvent yet more of my own lost Sam, I will never uncover the rumor of Jim Ezzelino. Mine is the sole case I can plead. Doesn't it always depend on the tale spinner? Take the teller from the story and what do you have but rootless formulation? So now I must set the old volume aside. For a few final pages I must delve only within myself. What is it? What is the story that I've come to tell myself, that comforts me, illuminates me, sets me to rest?

Now it is mostly just Barrett and the work we do about this alien village and our quiet nights.

But then it was the presence of the silent Sheherazade, the very fact that she was a woman; she brought some form of solace to me in my sad days recovering from a terrible year. The revelation of her sex, which sent me reeling when

I heard it first there on the plaza from the hysterically weeping red-haired Mrs. Bodman, finally released me from my torment. There she was. She still wore the clothes Sam had bought her, and so she must have looked the same to any innocent eye. But even the shearing of her black locks, rather than confirming her boyishness, only discovered her still deeper femininity. Was the delicate shape of her head now more clearly exposed? No, it was only in our minds that we saw her so differently, that we invested her with some entirely opposite aspect. Or did we realize, now, that we had never quite accepted her as a man either but had attributed our doubt to the unfamiliarity of her race? And even knowing what she was, it was hard to see her entirely as a woman of our own sort, either. Was it with such wonder and confusion that my own ancestors first commingled the blood of two continents centuries gone by?

There she sat by Otis Pond, the only residue of Sam's crusades, as if emerged from the epics he had read and now alive and eating and sleeping in our midst as proof of the existence of the outside world. In summer, when the time of the supple lady-slipper had given way to the time of Indian paintbrush and purple loosestrife, she wore her white tunic and baggy trousers and left her feet brown and bare, and her cropped hair lay close against her darkening brow, and her golden ring shone upon her left hand when the sun rose high enough to flood the sand where she sat so mournfully and peacefully and mute.

Sam had never loved a man. He could not have loved me as I'd wished him to. But, as I watched her, a strange sense grew in me that Sam, searching for some form of restitution, had come home to play the one part he had least fitted when he'd left us. He had humbled himself and placed his body where he'd remembered mine to have been. Of anyone in the village, he would now become most like me: he would bring a man to live with him. On his return, Sam had first embraced me, but I'd not known what to do. Sam couldn't have explained himself, wouldn't have, because he could only do and be, not say. Or, if he tried to say, in our language, he'd found his tongue had turned foreign. I didn't catch his masquerade (it was his mask as much as hers). But after some months of bereavement, the vision of their playfulness began to permeate my thoughts like candles gradually illuminating a room. Sam had shown himself like me in order to say he wished he could have loved me and never have hurt me and wished he could return to our young years to let me know. But no one can return like that.

It was September, the time of nodding asters ever returning, and I had been walking up the river in the late afternoon and come finally into the library I'd avoided all of the summer. Through the window I saw the woman from Arabia out there on our tiny desert by the pond, holding a twig in her hand, staring westward. The village was already getting used to her, accepting her insistence that she couldn't speak our language nor wished to learn it, but what would she do when winter came? We presumed Fred Otto would look out for her.

The Otto collection still entirely filled this library back then; Leota Colburn hadn't yet replaced our old Mrs. Collins. I sat down, not at this table where I'm writing but in my favorite chair there under the lamp, and tried to decide where I'd resume my reading after going some months without books. It was almost time. They were all waiting there. I could feel the spirit back in the room. Why it had left me after Landes's departure, I mean after Sam's death was less a question now than why I had let it leave. But here it was, trembling in the air again. But not quite yet. I would have to think a little more before I plunged.

Some child of the future, I thought, will fall among these dear volumes and read and come to know all that I know but perhaps understand more than I have understood.

O asters by the river road . . .